Penguin Books

CANDELO

Georgia Blain was born in Sydney in 1964.
She has worked as a journalist and copyright
lawyer. Her first novel, *Closed for Winter*, was
published in 1998.

GEORGIA BLAIN

candelo

PENGUIN BOOKS

Penguin Books Australia Ltd
487 Maroondah Highway, PO Box 257
Ringwood, Victoria 3134, Australia
Penguin Books Ltd
Harmondsworth, Middlesex, England
Penguin Putnam Inc.
375 Hudson Street, New York, New York 10014, USA
Penguin Books Canada Limited
10 Alcorn Avenue, Toronto, Ontario, Canada M4V 3B2
Penguin Books (NZ) Ltd
Cnr Rosedale and Airborne Roads, Albany, Auckland, New Zealand
Penguin Books (South Africa) (Pty) Ltd
4 Pallinghurst Road, Parktown 2193, South Africa

First published by Penguin Books Australia Ltd 1999

1 3 5 7 9 10 8 6 4 2

Text design by Nikki Townsend, Penguin Design Studio
Cover design by Ellie Exarchos, Penguin Design Studio
Typeset in 10.75/15 Berkeley Book by Midland Typesetters, Maryborough, Victoria
Made and printed in Australia by Australian Print Group, Maryborough, Victoria

National Library of Australia
Cataloguing-in-Publication data:

Blain, Georgia.
Candelo.

ISBN 0 14 027206 2.

I. Title.

A823.3

Many people have helped at various stages in the writing of this book. In particular I would like to thank Katrina, Louise and Anne for their insightful advice, and Anthony, Andre and Madeline for taking me back to Candelo.

Thank you also to Ali Watts and Julie Gibbs at Penguin, and Fiona Inglis from Curtis Brown.

Finally, a big thank you to Andrew and to the beautiful Odessa Stella, who came into our life just after the final edit was completed.

one

My mother, Violetta, has always believed that there is a division between right and wrong, that it is possible to draw a moral line.

I'm not talking about morality in a puritanical sense, she says, *nor am I talking about petty daily entanglements.*

And she isn't.

She is talking about something much larger than that. She is talking about the big issues, about taking a stand with an honest awareness of how each action will impact on the universal, about not being afraid to speak out, to battle for what you know to be right.

Simple, I say to her, with a certain measure of sarcasm.

She is usually easy to rail.

The problem with your generation, she tells me, *is that you expect others to do the fighting for you. You are quite happy to sit around and talk about what's wrong with the world, but you won't do anything about it – unless there's something in it for you.*

She beats her fist on the table. She is on a roll. *Look at*

1

feminism today, and she lifts her eyes to the ceiling in disgust. *There's no concept of united action. You get a modem, call yourself a grrrl and you never look beyond your own backyard.*

I tell her that I have never called myself a grrrl.

I should hope not, she says. She barely draws a breath before she continues. *What about cuts in health care? Education? Unemployment benefits? When was the last time you did anything other than sit around and complain? If you came to any of the few marches still being held, you'd see that it is predominantly my generation out there protesting.*

I wish I hadn't got her started.

Fighting for others has always been her life. For as long as I can remember. She sees inequality, she sees injustice and she is in there, battling for what she believes.

I'm not talking about the general, I say. *It's just that it is not always easy, on a personal level, to know what is right,* and as I speak, I can see her rolling her eyes. *If it isn't huge, if it isn't political, then it isn't real to you.*

She looks at me without blinking. *It certainly isn't of as much importance,* she says.

When Simon, my brother, came to tell me that Mitchell had died, I was, once again, enmeshed in the personal. And even in that arena, even in my own *petty daily entanglements,* I was managing to shift that line, draw it anywhere in the sand, and justify its placement to myself.

I was sitting on the back steps to our building and looking at the work I had made Marco do. Four days before I had asked him to move out.

2

It was during the last rains that the stairs had started sinking. As the mud slid down from the hill behind us, the bottom steps slipped with it. Already rotten, the wooden posts and landing began to shift, the boards breaking under the strain, leaving only a rickety backbone of what had once been there. Enough to tiptoe carefully, from upstairs to downstairs, but only just.

Like everything in this building, they remained unrepaired.

The owner, Mr Wagner, lives in Germany and we do not know how to contact him.

Mouse once told me that he left the country because he had buried a woman in the backyard, *under very sus circumstances*, and he winked, knowingly.

For whatever reason, we have never seen him. We just pay our rent into a bank account, and the disrepair continues. Even when it is as dangerous as those stairs were.

And that is how they would have stayed, if I hadn't begged Marco to fix them.

Why? he asked. *It's not like we ever go up there.*

I told him they were life threatening. That they, Anton or Louise, could kill themselves.

Well, let them do something about it, he said.

They won't, I told him.

And they wouldn't. Anton, I think, liked the romance of it all. He bought himself a rope ladder and kept it near the bathroom window. Louise was too obsessed with the slow dissolution of their relationship to notice.

When I wouldn't let up, Marco wanted to know why it concerned me so much.

I couldn't tell him the real reason. I couldn't tell him that I did, in fact, go up there. As often as I could. Waiting until he had gone off to work, waiting until I heard Louise's footsteps on the stairs and then, when it was all clear, knocking on their door.

I just kept on begging him, until, finally, he gave in. Four days before he packed the last of his few possessions into a box and carried it up the path to the road, slamming the door behind him as he told me that I would be sorry, that I would regret my decision. Marco fixed it all; all except the bottom step, which, still rotten, had collapsed into the dirt below.

And that is where I was sitting on the day my brother, Simon, came to tell me the news.

I had been sick again. A dull nausea that had left me unable to make it to my front door. Too listless to move, I was staring out past the coral trees, out past the morning glory, out past the sea, while from above me, I could hear them, Anton and Louise, arguing again.

I am sorry, Louise would say when she knocked on my door late at night after fights such as these. *I shouldn't bother you. But have you got a moment?*

And I would always let her in, my desire to know what was happening stronger than my ability to do what I knew was right. I would drink the scotch she had brought with her and I would watch the ice condense in the glass until the palm of my hand was cold and sweaty. Never lying but never telling the truth.

I heard the door slam upstairs, and I jumped.

I heard Anton tell her to calm down.

I heard her open the door and slam it again, the whole building shuddering with its impact, the windows rattling, the tremor travelling down the railing to the stairs as Anton no doubt shrugged his shoulders in helpless indignation at Louise's fury.

I began to pull myself up and, as I looked down at my feet, my ankles, my legs, cramped from sitting for too long, I failed to see him. My brother. Coming down the path towards me, the pale blue of his bus driver's shirt normally letting me know who it is before he arrives.

But not this time.

When I looked up, he was there.

And he had come to tell me that Mitchell had died.

two

Simon still lives at home with Violetta.

She used to worry that he would never leave. Now she just accepts the fact that he is there. Her house is large and their lives barely intersect.

In the past, their few exchanges of words were usually about the dishes, cleaning the bathroom, not leaving the laundry sitting in the washing machine for days. It was always Violetta directing the complaints, a staccato list as she rushed around the kitchen, tiny, bird-like in her high heels, picking up bowls, glasses, cups and never really putting them anywhere. Just shifting them, from one spot to the next. Sometimes Simon would look up from the paper and, not wanting any confrontation, quickly look down again.

Since my mother has been ill, Mari, who lives with her, has taken up the complaints. Not that she was silent in the past. But she would usually direct her frustration at Vi, telling her she could not bear it any longer. *He is a slob,* she would say. *For Christ's sake, Vi, he's a grown man. You shouldn't still be picking up after him.*

Once it became so bad that Mari packed her bags and told my mother that it was her or Simon. Violetta had to choose.

Don't make me do this, Violetta said.

She would, no doubt, have drawn back on her cigarette, then stubbed it out, half finished, before commencing to roll the next one. She would have told Mari she was being ridiculous. She would have promised she would talk to Simon.

And then, finding it all too difficult, she would have gone back to the report she was writing, 'The Sexuality of the Adolescent', or 'Crime, Children and Incarceration', or perhaps a piece for the paper, a book review, a speech.

Her notes would surround her and the ashtray would be overflowing. She would be immersed, unaware that Mari was packing the last of her bags, closing the door behind her, locking it and pushing the key through the letterbox. Unaware that Mari had, in fact, gone.

It is not that my mother does not care, it is just that she wouldn't have wanted to know. She would have waited, certain that a phone call would come. Or a knock on the door. Mari, wanting to pick up the rest of her things.

And when Mari did turn up, two maybe three days later, Vi would have stayed in her room while Mari cleared out the kitchen cupboards. Vi would have turned up the radio while Mari emptied the shelves, quietly at first and then, realising that Violetta was not going to come out and beg her to stay, more loudly, until she was dropping each pan on the floor, not once but twice, before she put it in the box.

It would only have been when the noise became unbearable that my mother would have opened her door. Clack, clack,

clack in her heels, furious at the disruption, both of them glaring at each other across the almost bare kitchen.

You're being ridiculous, Violetta would have said, arms folded.

Am I?

I've talked to Simon, and seeing that Mari was not going to waver, not without a little more, she would have told her that he had promised to change.

Hardly the words Mari had hoped for but at least they were some kind of start.

Please, because Vi would have known that it would not take much more. *There's no need for all of this.*

Not much of a reconciliation, but enough for Mari to stop her packing, just for a moment, and for my mother to reach out and touch her arm in the absent, barely there manner that she has.

Really? Mari would have asked.

Really, Vi would have said.

And in the silence that followed, they both would have looked away from each other, uncertain. Knowing that another move had to be made. Knowing it would be Mari; Mari who would look at Vi, who would tell her how awful she looked, like she hadn't slept, like she had been smoking too much, not eating, all of which would be true. Because this is the way my mother is. Whether Mari is there or not.

I am sorry, Mari would have finally said.

I am sorry too, and they would have stepped towards each other, still hesitant, still unsure as to whether the argument really was over, my mother drumming the tabletop with her fingers, wanting to light a cigarette but trying to stop herself.

Coffee? Mari would have asked.

And as Vi nodded, Mari would have begun to search for the percolator, unpacking the boxes on the floor at her feet.

It was all right; and my mother would have reached for her pouch of tobacco, her sigh of relief audible. Mari was home and life was, once again, normal.

Simon, no doubt, would have been completely unaware of the drama. It is unlikely my mother would have told him. Or perhaps he did know but he, too, just chose to ignore it, staying in his room and watching television or sleeping.

Like Vi, he is good at avoiding.

Simon and I are not close. We were once, but it seems so long ago, it is difficult for me to remember.

At the time of his visit, we only saw each other infrequently. Sometimes I would come home and he would be there, sitting outside my front door, smoking a cigarette and staring at the scuffs on his shoes. No doubt he had been there for hours, never thinking to call before he arrived, never thinking to just leave a note and go. He would wait, his shirt untucked from the creased cobalt blue of his bus driver's trousers, too tight, his stomach bulging out over his belt, his fingers nicotine stained, never without a cigarette, his eyes far away, staring at his shoes but seeing right past them, seeing something that only he can see.

He never comes for a reason. He just arrives. When I let him in, he is large and heavy in my small flat, filling the room that is my lounge and bedroom, not wanting anything to drink or eat, not even wanting to talk about anything in particular.

Instead, he will tell me in slow halting sentences about what happened on his route that day, or perhaps he will give me a run-down of an article he read in the paper, or a movie he watched on television, a blow-by-blow description of the plot, each scene described in excruciatingly dull detail.

I try to listen, but I soon find I am cleaning up around him, washing up, hinting that I have people coming over or I am going out, making phone calls to friends, until eventually he heaves himself up and sighs.

Well, I suppose I'd better go, he says.

As we part, as I watch him making his way back up the path, step by step, not even bothering to brush the oleander aside as it slaps into his face, I wish I had tried.

It is the gap between what he once was and what he has become.

The size of it. There in front of me.

And in the face of that, I am no good.

On that day, the day that Simon came to tell me Mitchell had died, he had not been over for almost two months.

I opened the windows wide in preparation for the thick yellow haze of smoke that would soon settle. He sat, heavily, in the armchair that had once belonged to our grandfather, thumbing through a script I had been reading for an audition.

It's a film, I told him, *a small part, but better than usual.*

He put it down.

He is not interested in my work. Nor is Violetta. But, in her case, this disinterest is a relief. The few times she has come to a play I have been in, she has sat right near the front, leaning forward, so that I can see her staring, I can feel her staring.

And afterwards, she tells me exactly what she thought. She tells me the script was didactic, the interpretation facile, the politics conservative, all the while drinking red wine and waving a cigarette in the air.

I put the script away and leant against the doorframe, one foot in, one foot out, looking out across the garden as I asked my brother how he was.

He told me he was okay, just the same, not much happening, and as I glanced towards him, I saw he was rubbing his hand nervously along the top of his thigh, unable to meet my eyes.

What's up? I asked him, and, frustrated, I turned away, rolling my eyes in irritation as I waited for him to speak.

You're so impatient, Marco would tell me when he saw me with Simon.

No I'm not, I would argue, but I would know he was right, and I would feel ashamed.

He's not that hard to talk to, he would say whenever I came home to find them both out in the garden, smoking cigarettes and seemingly managing to converse with ease; not once, but several times.

Just because he's a bus driver doesn't mean he has no opinions about the world, and Marco would raise his eyebrows to reinforce one of his favourite points: I was, and always would be, just too middle class.

And I would be furious with him.

From behind me, I could hear Simon clear his throat.

My brother's voice is soft. He often looks down as he talks; his words trail off as he realises that his attempts to be heard are floundering; half-finished sentences fall at his feet. He was answering me, but it was not just his uncertainty, nor just my failure to listen, it was the name that confused me, hearing it out loud after all those years, so that he had to say it again.

Mitchell.

And I was, for a moment, relieved. It wasn't Vi. It wasn't Bernard.

He wiped his forehead with the bottom of his shirt and, despite the cool, I could see that he was hot. Clammy. The perspiration condensing near his hairline.

What happened? I asked, my surprise at the mention of Mitchell's name only just beginning to register.

I waited for him to speak. In the silence, I could hear them above me, Anton and Louise. She was sweeping the floor of the flat. This is what she does when she is agitated. He was helping her move the furniture. This is what he does when he feels guilty.

Simon, too, glanced upwards.

I watched him swallow, followed by the hesitant scratch of a cough. Wiping his nose with the back of his hand.

I want to go to the funeral, and I could barely hear him. *I want to go to the funeral,* he said again, lifting his head now and looking straight at me.

I did not want him to say what I knew he was going to say next. I guessed before he even spoke the words, before he even asked me if I would go with him. And I looked straight back at my brother and told him that I didn't want to go.

Not to Mitchell's funeral. Not to that.

three

I do not know how Mitchell was when they took him away.

He may have hung his head, his long blond hair stiff with salt and falling into his eyes as they put his hands behind his back.

He may have been silent, knowing there was no point, staring at the gravel underfoot as they walked him back up the incline towards the road, towards the waiting car. Or he may have shouted and screamed, struggled, swore at them to keep their fucking hands off him, as they pushed him into the back, slamming the door behind him.

I do not know whether he was scared.

There on the back seat, the vinyl sticky beneath his skin, one thin leg jiggling up and down, up and down, the slap of his heel against his thong, over and over again. Staring out the window. Nothing but the black hills and the white of the headlights as they turned back onto the road and drove away from that place.

I have always imagined they were the last to leave the scene.

But that may not have been how it was.

Down by the creek bed, dry at this part, there may have been others. Wrapping chains around my mother's car, the clank of metal on metal, the groan and grind of the truck engine and the scrape of the body against the boulders, as they hauled and heaved it up to the road.

And in the hot stillness of that night, they might have stopped to wipe the sweat off their faces, the black grease from a singlet smeared across a forehead. In the sharp beam of the light from the truck, they might have seen how crushed the metal was and looked at each other.

Amazing any of them survived, one might have said, not expecting a response. Turning back to the task. Knowing they were just words, words about an accident that hadn't really touched on their lives, that would soon be forgotten, words left to drift out in the dark closeness of that valley.

Bloody amazing, the policeman might also have said. Same words, somewhere else. Words that were not left to drift. Words that came down hard. Hard as the fist on the desk.

So, what have you got to say for yourself? And as he leant forward, waiting for an answer, expecting an answer, I can only guess how Mitchell might have responded.

I can only guess how Mitchell might have felt.

Because, the truth is, I never really knew him.

The truth is, none of us did.

It was Vi who brought Mitchell into our lives. About fifteen years ago.

She would deny that, if we talked about him, which we don't.

14

She would say that it was a democratic process. That we all had a chance to have our say. That we took a vote.

I always listened to you, she says. *I always took your views into consideration.*

And, on the surface, she did.

Whenever there was a decision to be made, an issue that would affect us all, Vi would call a house meeting. It did not matter whether the question was large or small, Vi would put it to a vote. And somehow, the numbers always stacked in her favour.

We discussed Mitchell three days before we were due to go on holiday.

It is important, Vi told us, *that we learn to share a little of what we have,* and she waved her arm in the air to indicate all that we possessed, *with others. I don't think the three of you realise just how fortunate you are.*

She laid a couple of badly typed sheets onto the table in front of us. I could only just make out the heading on one – 'The Desmond Halls Placement Program'.

It has been set up, Vi explained, *to ease adolescents from institutions, foster homes or disadvantaged families into adulthood. It's for kids who are about to look after themselves.*

She picked up the bottom sheet and started reading out loud. *Ideally, the program will work as a give and take experience. It's not only the adolescent who will benefit from their stay with the placement family, but the family themselves.*

We looked at her.

Do any of you have anything you'd like to say?

Simon looked at his watch. He wanted to get back to the

Stewarts' house. *Sounds okay to me,* he said, which was how he responded to most of Vi's proposals. Evie said she needed to go to the toilet, and I said I didn't want a stranger on our holidays. *Not at all,* I added, in case I hadn't been heard the first time.

And I didn't. I wanted us to have time with Vi. Away from her work.

I'm disappointed in you, and she poured herself another glass of red wine, and pushed the bottle towards Simon and me. *In fact, I really wouldn't have expected it,* and as she looked at me through her reading glasses, she cut herself a piece of cheese from the stale block she always brought out for these meetings. *Why?* she asked.

I could not think of a valid justification. Not a single one.

Well, not in her eyes anyway.

I think we're all agreed, then, she said, and it was clear that the decision had been made.

When I told my father about the holiday, he made little effort to hide his disinterest.

Really, he said, but I could hear him on the other end of the telephone telling his new girlfriend, Jane, that he didn't want any salad with his meal. Not yet, he liked it afterwards, on a different plate.

You're not listening, I told him.

I am, darling, I am.

But he wasn't.

You know what your mother's like, and he tried to reassure me. *Just humour her. Let it be. It won't be so bad.*

He had given up on Vi's passions a long time ago. I doubt

whether he was ever really that interested, although she assures me that he was.

He changed, she tells me with some disgust.

Bernard is a QC. When they met, he was instrumental in setting up the first community legal centres. *God knows what happened to him,* Vi says, and it is clear that she wants to change the topic.

Simon, too, didn't care. Not all that much.

It's no big deal, he told me.

I tried: *But if you came with me, and said you didn't want him, then it would be two of us. Against one. We could ask for a re-vote.*

He wasn't interested.

And Evie was too young.

There was no point.

So, that was the way it stacked up.

That was the way it always stacked up.

Mitchell was dead and Simon wanted me to go to his funeral.

Why? I asked him and he did not answer.

I could only guess that it was some act of forgiveness. A gesture. A peacemaking. And I did not want to participate.

I stood in my doorway, listening to the clatter of plates from the flats next door, dinner being prepared, the low hum of television from the flats behind them, the sound of a car pulling out from the flats on the other side, and, from above me, from our own block, silence. I turned to go inside and then, faced with the emptiness in front of me, found myself stepping back into the garden, back to where the stairs down the cliff once began, and still were if you hacked your way through the knotted vines and sticky lantana, back to where I could see up to their windows. Lights on, curtains open, and the strain of the rusted sashes with each faint stir of breeze.

Evening. Mouse raised his hand in greeting as he walked past, his smirk just visible in the dark. He knew what I was doing.

I did not bother responding.

He had locked himself out again and I watched as he forced his window open and started climbing through, head first.

I willed him to get stuck.

Or at least fall, hard, onto the floor below.

Lost your key? I asked him.

There's no rule that says you gotta use the door, and he slammed the window behind him, the glass rattling in the pane.

I was alone again. There was nothing to see. Nothing to hear. And I suddenly felt foolish.

Inside, I sat by my window and I tried not to think about Mitchell. The pages of the script were open in front of me, but I kept on looking out to the lights of the houses on the north point. Despite what I had said to Simon, the film was dull and tedious.

I was being auditioned to play a heroin addict. This is the type of part that I am always offered. Probably because, like Violetta, I am small and thin with dark circles under my eyes. As I closed the script, I saw myself, there in the reflection of the window, and I looked away.

It was not just Mitchell I was trying not to think about.

It was myself. It was the situation I was in.

I saw my reflection and I saw why the doctor had been concerned when I had gone to see her that morning.

You need to make sure you get plenty of iron, she had said, *if you're going to go ahead with this.*

She had given me a card for a clinic. And a letter of referral.

Give yourself a couple of weeks, she had said, *before you make any decisions.*

I picked up the telephone and then, halfway through dialling Vi's number, I hung up. I wasn't ready to speak to her yet. I didn't know what I would say, how I would attempt to explain the situation in which I had found myself.

I dialled another number.

Lizzie had friends over. I could hear someone laughing in the background, the clatter of cutlery falling to the floor.

It was not a good time to talk.

On the weekend, she promised.

And as I rolled myself a joint, I promised myself I would stop smoking if and when I made my decision.

But until then, if I was going to sleep, I needed all the help I could get.

four

Once, a long time ago, Simon had a lot of friends.

Always late home from school, he would drift from a neighbour's house to the corner, and then on to the park, perhaps the newsagency; unaware of the time, even with the first flicker of the streetlights, he would simply forget he was meant to be home.

Vi would always tell me to go and find him.

And I would.

Always wanting to be where he was, to be part of whatever it was that the older kids did, I would know where to look for him. At the bowling green smoking cigarettes, his short pockets stuffed with stolen chalk, on the oval trying to throw boomerangs and get them to come back, out on the street playing handball, perhaps at someone's house, stoned and listening to records; it never took me long to track him down.

I would come in and tell him dinner was ready. Now.

He would look up, surprised.

But it's only five, he would say.

I would roll my eyes and show him my watch.

Unaware of how late it was, he would just be wherever he was. Completely.

And that was what drew people to him. That, and the gentleness in his nature.

You could not help but like him.

Simon no longer has the friends he used to have. There is really only myself and Vi. And we are his family.

I once asked Vi what she thought had happened to him. Why the change had occurred. But as soon as I articulated the question, I wished I hadn't. I knew I had led us into a territory that neither of us had the heart to enter.

I watched as she tried to light a match, as it splintered against the flint and failed to catch. She tried three times before she spoke, drawing back sharply on her cigarette and staring out the window, as she told me she didn't know.

It's just the way he is, she said and she did not turn to look at me.

I did not press it any further.

Because when it comes to Simon, it seems as though we constantly fail, as though inaction is the path we choose.

The morning after he came to me with his news, I did not call Vi, dreading the prospect of mentioning Mitchell's name but knowing it had to be done. I did not call my father and arrange to meet him for lunch that day. I did not ask him to speak to Simon.

I did not do anything.

I just learnt my lines, repeating them to myself in the mirror as I cleaned the bathroom that is shared by both the downstairs flats. Mine and Mouse's.

I scrubbed the toilet until there was not a trace of Mouse's footprints left. He likes to squat. *It's what they do in India,* he tells me whenever I complain.

I cleaned the tiles around the shower until they were sparkling.

I washed down the floor.

I wiped the basin until it gleamed.

And I played out my entire scene five times.

When I was finished, when I had learnt all I had to learn, I dumped the dirty sponges at Mouse's door, and I waited for Louise to go to work, for her footsteps down the stairs.

Louise is a sub-editor. She works shifts. When she is on the morning shift, she leaves at eight, when she is on the afternoon shift, two, and the evening shift, nine. I knew these times by heart. I still know them.

That morning she was late, and I stood, nervously, there on that bottom step, unsure as to whether I should go up, unsure as to whether I should knock on their door in the hope she had already left.

Louise does not like her job. She has told me this often. They moved to this city a year ago, and she was forced to take whatever was available.

It was Anton who wanted to come here, she once said, brushing her hair out of her face and then letting it fall back again. *He thought there would be more opportunity, for his scripts,* and she sighed. *But he is still broke and I am still supporting him.*

She would tell me she had no one else with whom she

22

could talk. *I hope you don't mind,* she would say as I opened the door to her standing awkward, unsure, a bottle in one hand, a pack of cigarettes in the other.

Once she told me Anton's work hadn't been the only reason for the move. *I had a miscarriage,* she said. *I kind of fell apart.*

Another time she told me it was because Anton had had an affair, and she had looked at me, just for a moment, as she poured herself another drink.

Who knows? Marco said when I asked him what he thought the real reason was, and he looked up impatiently from the pile of notes he had brought home to read. *Who cares?*

He always found Louise irritating. He had little patience for her endless talk about her problems. It was self-indulgent.

Bourgeois, I would say to tease him.

Precisely, he would say, but he would usually smile back.

He had even less time for Anton. *A sleaze-bag,* and he would not look at me. *A spoilt rich kid dabbling in the arts.*

And each time he heard the footsteps from upstairs followed by a knock on our door, he would roll his eyes. *Don't,* he would mouth silently as I would get up, ignoring him, opening the door to see her standing there.

I looked up to the landing at the top of the stairs and closed my front door behind me.

Before you make any kind of decision, you should talk to him, the doctor had told me, and I had nodded my head as though it was a given.

In the closed stillness of the corridor outside their flat, I knocked once, hoping she had somehow gone without me hearing her.

But she hadn't.

She was the one who answered the door. She was the one with whom I talked. The two of us, out on the landing, Louise picking at splinters in the wood, staring down at her feet as she told me they had been fighting again.

I wish I had the courage to just go, she said, her voice hushed, quiet, because she did not want him to hear. Anton, just one thin wall away. *I wish I was more like you. You just took action. It wasn't working and you made your decision.*

And she looked out across the overgrown garden, out across the low shrubs that cling to the side of the hill behind these flats, their roots gripping the sandy soil, only just, as she told me how lonely she felt.

If it wasn't for you, I don't know what I would do, and she lit a cigarette, holding it awkwardly in her left hand, the smoke drifting up and into my eyes. *He tells me I'm mad. And now I'm starting to think I am. Now I'm starting to wonder whether I have just been imagining that he's up to his old tricks,* and I watched as she scratched the end of the match into the wooden railing, one thin black line. *Perhaps I have just made it all up. Perhaps he does still love me.*

And she flicked her ash down into the garden.

He says he does.

I was silent.

And why shouldn't I believe him?

I did not answer her and I did not meet her gaze.

She thanked me for coming up. She thanked me for coming to see if she was all right. Because when she opened the door, I had told her that I just wanted to know if she was okay.

Speaking softly, knowing he was there, just on the other side of the wall.

I appreciate it, she said, as I told her I had to get going, that I was late for work.

I turned to the stairs, the stairs I had made Marco fix, and she watched as I made my way back down to my flat. I could not see her, but I knew she was still there, leaning on the railing, watching me, the ash from her cigarette floating down, drifting past me, and into the garden below.

And I wished I had been able to speak to him.

That it was over and done with.

And not the unknown, still to be faced.

five

─────────

You see, Vi says to me, *the personal is, by and large, a distraction. A self-indulgent excuse.*

I drum my fingers on the table. Loudly.

I am not saying always. But often. We get embroiled in trying to make our lives measure up to petty fantasies and we ignore the larger issues in life.

When she talks like this, I try to stay calm, but more often than not, I fail. I want to tell her that in her case, the global seems to be the distraction, the way of hiding from the personal. But if I begin to voice this, she gets furious.

You are being ridiculous, she says. *I always gave my utmost to the three of you. I don't think you could ever say that I neglected you. You were enormously privileged,* and she lowers her glasses so that she is looking me straight in the eye.

I cannot explain to her that this was not what I meant.

If ever a choice needed to be made, ever, and she pauses as she pushes her glasses back up onto the bridge of her nose, *I always chose my children.*

She shakes her head and I can see how much I have upset her. *I loved you all,* she says. *I still do.*

I see the dark circles under her eyes, her grey skin, soft, paper thin when I kiss her cheek, and I feel ashamed for having criticised her.

I tell her that I know she does.

But as I reach for her hand, I wish it didn't always end like this. I wish we could sometimes speak of the things we need to talk about.

Like the decision I was trying to make at the time of Mitchell's funeral.

Like Mitchell himself.

The fact that his name had remained unmentioned for so long, the fact that none of us had seen him or spoken to him for all those years, did not mean I couldn't picture him. With my eyes closed, he was there.

Mitchell Jenkins.

His bag at his feet. The zip broken, a pair of underpants, leopard print, sticking out of the opening. The dust coating his feet dirty grey.

I looked at him from the ground upwards.

Tall, thin and slightly bow-legged. Tight jeans, thongs and a checked shirt, sleeves rolled up to tanned forearms. Dark eyes looking at us, the three of us, through a fall of long blond hair. Looking at us and grinning.

This, Vi said, *is Mitchell,* and she turned to us. *This,* she said, *is Simon, Ursula and Evie.*

He held out his hand and the smile widened. Impossible in

its breadth. Challenging the wariness that was, without doubt, evident in our faces.

Gidday, and he turned to each of us, one by one.

But it wasn't just his smile that I saw; it was his foot tapping, his mouth chewing gum, the fingers of his other hand clenched against his thigh; these small signs of nervousness beneath the bravado of that grin.

And I did not give an inch.

Simon, however, reached out to return the greeting, shy for a moment, awkward, as their grasp missed and then caught.

I just met his gaze. Without a word. And in the silence that followed, I watched as he kicked his feet in the dirt, as he scratched a hole with the toe of his thong, and as he kept on staring at me, seemingly unperturbed by my failure to acknowledge him, until, with a further widening of that grin, he finally turned to Evie.

It's not 'gidday', she told him, mimicking Vi's own words to us each time we lapsed into any semblance of lingo. *It's 'hello'.*

Vi glared at her.

That's what you say to us, and she crossed her arms obstinately.

All the time, I added, but under my breath.

And Simon kicked me, hard, on the shin.

Mitchell had been to four foster homes. He didn't tell us this. Nor did Vi. I read it in the letter from the placement program.

When I asked her why, I knew the answer I was going to get. A lecture about disadvantages. About abuse. About single mothers. About poverty. All punctuated by sharp, angry taps of her cigarette against the side of the ashtray.

What I wanted to know was whether he'd ever been in trouble, serious trouble.

Vi told me to stop being childish. *Mitchell's past is Mitchell's business,* and she turned back to her work. *Stop being difficult and give it a try.*

I looked offended. I told her that of course I would. Who did she think I was?

But I didn't. Not at first. I remember.

We were hot and cramped in the back seat. Simon, Evie and I pressed against each other, sticky skin on sticky skin, furnace blasts of air rushing in through the open window, while in the front, Mitchell stretched out and tapped his fingers on the dashboard in time to whatever tape he had put into the cassette player, singing out of tune to whatever song happened to be playing.

Reckon I've got a voice? he asked Vi in all seriousness, and I saw her looking at him, uncertain as to how to respond.

The white of his teeth was reflected in the rear-vision mirror as he caught my eye and smiled.

Pretty bad, hey? and his look was sheepish, but he did not stop. He just turned the volume up another notch and sang a little louder, grinning with embarrassment whenever his attempts to hit the note went blatantly wrong.

How come he's allowed to choose what we listen to? I asked Vi at the service station. *And how come we have to listen to that?* I added, referring to his singing.

It wasn't that I hated what he put on. In fact it was a relief from the usual Joan Baez or Harry Belafonte that Vi always played, and I had to admit that his singing was amusing us all.

It was the unfairness of it. Simon and I were never allowed to play our tapes in the car. We always brought them with us, but they stayed in the glove box.

Mitchell hadn't even asked. One push of the eject button and Joan Baez was back in her case, replaced by David Bowie.

I had looked at Simon. I had waited for Vi's response.

Nothing. Simon had just shrugged his shoulders and Vi hadn't seemed to notice.

You never let us play our tapes, I complained to Vi as we waited at the counter.

She pushed her sunglasses up into her hair and searched for her money in her purse. She was ignoring me. But I was not going to be stopped.

How come he can?

Do you want a drink? she asked.

No, I told her.

Just as well, she said, and she held out her hand for the change.

I looked at her.

Because I certainly wasn't going to buy you one, and she turned her back on me, leaving me standing by the cash register, still waiting for an answer to my question.

Back in the car, Simon and Mitchell had swapped seats. Leaning forward into the front, Mitchell talked constantly. Asking endless questions about where we were going, the places we drove through and what Simon liked to do. Music, skateboards and surfing. He wanted to know everything. Comparing bands they liked, food, movies. He barely stopped to catch air as he leapt from topic to topic.

But it was the surfing that fascinated him the most. He had never done it before.

You surf, Ursula? and Mitchell was looking at me, grinning again.

No, I said, defiant, determined not to give him an entry, although I could see the exclusion that was going to occur. Him and Simon. Me and Evie. It was stacking up.

So what do you do? he asked.

I told him that there were other things in the world besides surfing. That I couldn't believe the ignorance of his question.

He just kept smiling, and as his dark-brown eyes focused on mine, I could feel myself beginning to smile in response, my mouth turning up at the sides. I could not help myself. But then I saw them, Vi staring at me in the rear-vision mirror, and Simon, sitting next to her and glaring, and I became all the more determined not to relent in my behaviour. Not in front of them.

When we stopped for an ice-cream, Simon told me I shouldn't be so rude. *Imagine how he feels,* and my brother's eyes were wide with compassion. *There's all of us and only him.*

He'll cope, I told him, irritated with the way he was always on the side of the underdog. Irritated with how well he and Mitchell seemed to be getting on.

And I rolled my eyes in disgust as I heard him, Mitchell, hamming it up, yet again.

Jeez, he said as Vi passed him a Cornetto, *never had such a classy ice-cream.*

Evie couldn't believe it. I looked at Simon, but he had turned away.

Reckon the last time I had an ice-cream was . . . and he paused for effect, *four years ago.*

Really? Evie stared at him. Impressed. Completely and utterly.

True, he answered, solemn, pitiful, to an extreme.

Back in the car, Simon stayed in the front seat, Mitchell in the back. Evie was sandwiched between us. Separating us. But I could still see his long thin legs in his tight jeans. The left jiggling up and down. Up and down. The tapping of his hand on his knee.

Vi put her Joan Baez back into the cassette player. Simon did not even attempt to change it, but I wasn't prepared to let things rest, not even from the back seat. I asked Simon to put Pink Floyd on. He waited for Vi's response. I waited for Vi's response.

I think we'll have something a little more peaceful for a while, she said.

See, I told her.

She ignored me.

And on we went.

Eight hours south. Hugging the coast. Small seaside towns with winding main streets. A pub, a post office, and a milk bar. Slow traffic clogging up each entrance and then dispersing out on the highway. Holding my breath each time Vi overtook a truck, clutching the steering wheel, foot flat on the floor, swearing loudly as she willed the car to go faster, faster. Swinging around a bend and being flung to the other side of the seat, Mitchell's side, where I would have been pressed tight against him if it weren't for Evie separating us. Just. And as I pushed myself up again, I could not help but touch him. There

32

was no space for me to do anything else. My hand was forced onto his leg.

He looked at me, at where my skirt had ridden up my thighs.

And I looked at him, at where my palm had rested on his knee.

And he grinned, yet again, his dark eyes resting momentarily on mine.

We drove until it was dark, turning off the highway into the quiet of the country night, onto a narrow road that twisted and turned inland. It was too early for the stars, and the sky overhead was black, unbroken by lights. Nothing but the sound of the engine. Evie was asleep, Simon was asleep and Mitchell was asleep. Vi was hunched forward over the steering wheel, and in the reflection of the rear-view mirror, I could see how tired she was, the match flaring as she lit another cigarette, her face ghoulish in the momentary flame.

But it was not her I watched.

It was Mitchell.

His head rolled to one side so that all I could see was his profile, half hidden by the long blond hair. His eyelashes, dark and thick, twitching slightly as he dozed. His wide mouth, soft, his lips pale against his tan. His hands resting on his thighs, square and brown, the nails bitten down, and on his index finger, a long jagged scar.

When Vi pulled over for the second time, it was clear that she did not know where we were.

We all woke up, all of us except Evie, who stayed where she was, her head tucked into Mitchell's side as he leant forward to take the map from Vi.

Jesus, and his mouth was wide open as he stared out the window, forgetting the map for one brief moment, as he gazed out across the black of the country to the sky, *look at them all.*

I leant across Evie so that I could see, out past the reflection of his eyes in the window, to the thousands of stars now spread across the sky.

That's what it's like away from the city, Vi told him.

No kidding, and he shook his head in amazement as he spread the map out and traced the line of where we had been with the tip of his finger. I watched him as he paused for a moment, still stunned by the beauty of what he had seen, before telling us we were on the right road. *Shouldn't be much further,* he said.

And he was right.

It wasn't.

Candelo. Right around the next bend.

six

Anton was not my first lie.

But most of the untruths I had told before were small in comparison: white lies, telling friends I liked their work when I had slept through their performance, saying I was sick when I didn't want to go somewhere, breaking up with lovers and telling them I wanted to be friends when I knew, without a doubt, that this was the last thing I wanted.

These are the lies I tell.

These are the lies most people tell.

Marco, on the other hand, found it difficult to tell even these lies. He would say that he believed, always, in the truth; his eyes intent, earnest, the expression on his face one of utmost seriousness, as he explained what to him was an important principle.

But I would watch as his attempts at honesty led him into awkward complications and I would become impatient.

Just lie, I would say. *It doesn't matter.*

It did to him. Or so he said. Because sometimes I cannot

help but wonder whether he clung steadfast to those small truths as a ballast against the greater lie that had grown between the two of us.

Simon, too, does not lie.

Once, we broke Vi's favourite vase. The tennis ball flying too high through the air, out of reach, it hit the table and bounced to the ground, the vase clattering after it.

The glue sticky beneath my fingers, I tried to put the pieces back together, to align rose with rose, thorn with thorn. But there was no point.

Simon told Vi as soon as she came in the door. And as he held it up to show her, she said that it was not the breakage that upset her, but my attempt to conceal it.

She was just trying to fix it, Simon offered.

It was no use.

Simon was honest and I was punished.

With my brother, it is only ever truth or silence. And when he chooses silence he is stubborn, immovable.

My father, however, is a consummate liar.

One of the best, Vi says, and she does not attempt to hide her disgust.

It was my father who got me the job I had at that time, the job I still have. A part-time position. Receptionist in a law firm.

Ursula is an actor, he tells people proudly. *Excellent on the telephone. Excellent voice,* and when he suggests me for work, I usually get it. People know it is in their interest to do him a favour.

There is never a lot to do. I type letters, make coffee for meetings, order flowers, book restaurants and file. And in the gaps between tasks, I try to learn an audition piece, to read, to do anything but just stare out the window and let the boredom seep in.

On my first day of work, I was told that I was not allowed to make personal calls.

You must be available to answer the phone after three rings only. Always, and I had nodded to show that I understood. But it was rare that I kept to the rule. And on that day, the day after I learnt of Mitchell's death, I broke it, repeatedly.

In each quiet moment, I called Anton. Number by number. Hanging up halfway through as the realisation of what I would have to say hit me, catching a glimpse of myself in the glass doors and wondering what words I would manage to find.

Anton loves the telephone. When he is trying to work, he turns the volume on both the phone and the answering machine right down, and then covers them with pillows. When it rings, he runs his fingers through his thick curly hair and sighs impatiently, but it is obvious that he is listening, straining to hear the message, and just as the caller is about to hang up, he will lunge for the receiver.

Wait, he would say to me.

I won't be long, he would promise, his hand resting on my arm, asking me to stay.

And I would wait, stealing glances at Louise's half-read books, spines bent back and left lying open on the floor, each one discarded with the next one started, while I tried to listen to what he was saying.

Anton loves to talk, to tell stories. Stories about his travels, his impossible love affairs, the latest mess he has found himself in, and with each tale he will shrug his shoulders helplessly as he says he doesn't understand, just doesn't understand, how it happened.

He would settle back in the chair, light a cigarette, and I would know that it wouldn't just be a matter of a few minutes. An ex-girlfriend, an old friend, a project officer from a funding agency – he would talk endlessly, his tales more elaborate with each telling. And despite knowing what he was, despite knowing that I, too, was another mess he had stumbled into, I could not resist him. I would keep going back. I would knock on his door and I would kiss him. Straightaway. Drinking in the warmth of his breath. The sea breeze through the open windows, sometimes gentle, sometimes strong enough to pull the door, slam, shut behind me, cupboard doors opening and closing, opening and closing, and the curtains lifting and falling, as I would tell him I had just come up to see him. That was all.

And he would look at me, helpless, charming. *I shouldn't be doing this,* he would say, *but you keep seducing me.*

I looked out across the city spread below me, still and distant, and I dialled his number again, this time right through, only to hang up before his telephone rang. I looked at the tulips I had arranged in the vase this morning and wished I had chosen another flower. They were already overblown, the tip of one leaf brown.

I wished I knew him better. I wished it hadn't come to this. I wished I could trust him with what I had to say.

And I couldn't imagine how I would even begin to find the first word that I needed.

Once when I was in high school, I phoned a boy seventeen

times in one night, putting down the phone each time he answered. He had been my boyfriend. He had started seeing my best friend. His parents complained to the school that someone was making nuisance calls. They suspected it was a student. Could they do something about it?

The teacher made an announcement in class. A warning to the person who had been *pulling this stunt* that it was not on. *Just not on.*

Everyone knew it was me.

But I did not bat an eyelid. I did not flinch, despite knowing that each and every student in the class was looking at me, waiting to see how I would react. I just looked straight back at the teacher.

I had been furious with him, and I had felt completely justified in what I had done. It was, after all, nothing compared to what he had done to me.

But it was not fury that made me keep dialling Anton's number, hanging up two, maybe three numbers in, sometimes just before the answering machine clicked on to Louise's voice, and then trying again, in each lull during the day, knowing that the light on the switch had been red far too often for the managing partner's liking.

I'm sorry, I told him, *about all these calls. It's my boyfriend,* I explained. *He's very ill and I've been anxious about him. He hasn't been answering.*

He looked at me with concern.

Perhaps you should go home? he suggested.

I reassured him that it was fine. *He's probably just asleep,* I said.

39

When's the next audition? he asked me, wanting to appear more friendly, more relaxed, because this is the image he likes to present and he is, after all, one of my father's best friends.

I told him it was the next morning. *Another junkie,* I said and he laughed. Like most people, he has only ever seen a short stint I once had in a soap opera. A slow death from an AIDS-related illness.

One day, I said, *I will get to play someone who is together. Perhaps even glamorous, rich and powerful.*

Maybe even a lawyer, he laughed.

Maybe even a lawyer, I agreed.

Good luck, he said.

And when he walked off, I left a message for Simon at the bus depot and I tried Anton one more time, closing my eyes as I listened to Louise's message, as I let it play right through, as I paused at the end of the beep, and then, faced with the silence, found myself without words.

I hung up.

I would go and see him tomorrow.

I would talk to him then.

seven

A river cut the town in two. A river that wound its way through the valley, twisting across the only way in, slicing right through the middle of the small cluster of houses and shops, and then twisting once more so that you had to cross it yet again as you left.

Three bridges. All of which have flooded and will, no doubt, flood again.

The year before we went to Candelo, it was the bridge that joined one side of the town to the other that went. Swept away as the water rose, the river choking the banks as it crept up the wide trunks of the great elms planted at the edge, forcing its way higher until the pylons eventually collapsed under the strain.

Three years before that it was the bridge that took you out of there, onto the road that leads up to the high Monaro country, where the tufts of grass lie flattened by the wind and the gums pierce the sky.

And once all three went down. No way in. No way out. No way across.

Candelo.

Cut off from everyone else, and cut off from itself.

It was Mitchell who navigated the last stretch, directing us across the bridge that joined two shadowy ribbons of pub, general store, police station and houses, all circled by dense hills, into one.

First left, he told Vi, following the road on the map in front of him, his hair illuminated by the single light in the roof of the car.

Are you sure? she asked him, knowing she had given him the responsibility in an attempt to make him feel part of the family, but uncertain as she always was when she handed any form of control to another. She had looked at the map earlier and she was sure it had been right.

No, it's left, Mitchell said and he passed the map to Simon for confirmation, their shoulders touching as they bent towards each other to look.

He's right, Simon said, as Vi clicked the indicator on to right.

She paused for a moment and Simon leant across the steering wheel and flicked the switch back up. *It's left,* he said again.

True, Mitchell nodded, clearly amused by the whole performance.

And Vi shook her head in resignation, as she turned in a direction that she was certain was wrong.

There was a shudder as we hit the dirt, and Simon told Evie she should put her thumb on the window. *Stops it shattering.*

She did as she was told, the warmth of her body stretched

42

across my lap, her other thumb still in her mouth.

It wasn't far. Ten minutes out of town. The scrap of paper Vi had brought with her, instructions from the people who had lent us the house, told us it was about five miles. But in the darkness, lost in the first folds of the hills, it felt as though we were miles from anywhere.

Next bend should be the drive, Mitchell told us.

And it was. There, on our left, the rusted cattle grate marking the entrance, illuminated for a moment by the headlights as Vi slowed down to take the dip, so that we saw, for that one instant, the body flung over the grate, limp with no sheen in the scales.

Snake, and Mitchell was out of the car before it had even stopped, the front door slamming as Simon followed.

Don't, Vi called after him, but it was too late.

He was gone. There with Mitchell, startlingly bright in the headlights, as they picked up the long body and held it high for us to see.

It's a fucking whopper. And in the still of the night, Mitchell's voice rang out, loud and broad, as he put the tail in Simon's hands and held the head in his own, both of them stretching out the body to its full length.

I had seen my brother with death before.

I had heard him wake in the middle of the night, screaming, his pet rabbit cold in his hands, suffocated when he had rolled over to where it always slept, next to him. I had seen him turn his back on a dead bird washed up on the beach, his face white with fear, as I dared him to pick it up.

And I saw him then with a dead snake stretched out in his hands.

With all his attention focused on Mitchell, he was seemingly unaware of what he was doing. His gaze was shy, uncertain, as he stood there in front of us, the body now slack between them.

Hsss, and Mitchell bared his teeth and flicked out his tongue.

Simon laughed and I was surprised.

Hsss, and it was only as Mitchell dropped the head, as it hit the dust and Simon was left bearing the weight alone, that there seemed to be a moment of realisation.

I saw him wince, the tail slipping between his fingers, his eyes uncertain as he stared straight into the headlights, straight at Mitchell getting back into the car.

Vi turned the key in the ignition, the car rattling as we crossed the grate, the rear end slumping low, almost scraping the metal, before we were back on the dirt, the road potholed and steep as it led down to the creek and beyond that the house.

It was the trees that we saw first.

Cypresses, thick and dark, marking out the borders of what had once been a garden. The remains of a wooden gate, which was left slung low off its hinges. The road at an end, just thick long grass leading up to the black of the house.

We did not know what to expect. But this was what it was like when we went on holidays with Vi. Driving miles to strange places, places offered to her by people she did not know. People who admired her work, who thought she might need a break; somewhere to finish a paper she had to write, somewhere quiet. Places that often proved to be uninhabitable, but occasionally proved to be more than we had hoped for. And as the car pulled up alongside the verandah, I had my fingers crossed, tight, willing something better than what I suspected we would find. Hoping it would be all right, as Vi searched for the key, the contents of her bag strewn across her lap, her door open so that she could see by the indoor light.

Nothing.

She swore loudly.

I haven't forgotten them, she told us, directing her comment at me in particular. *I just can't find them,* defensive before I even had a chance to get impatient with her.

She passed me her bag, and I began to search. Rummaging through cigarette packs, matches, loose money, scraps of paper with telephone numbers, but no keys. A chaos that used to drive my father crazy.

Not here, I told her, trying to keep the triumph out of my voice.

Maybe there's an open window, Simon suggested.

But it was Mitchell who got out of the car. *This is when you need someone like me.* And he looked at each of us, his eyes wide and innocent. *Anyone got a crowbar?*

Simon opened his own door, eager to follow, eager to be a part of whatever it was that Mitchell intended to do, and the pair of them ran across the grass and up the stairs to the verandah.

It was the fuse box that Mitchell wanted. It creaked as he prized it open, the lid clanging shut as he bent the fuse wire to the shape he needed, and, calling Simon over, proceeded to show him how to pick a lock.

Piece a cake, he told him, and just as Vi accidentally knocked the volume on the radio, the dramatic strains of a requiem blasting out into the quiet of the night, the front door swung open with the force of both their bodies.

Jesus fucking Christ. Fucking Jesus, Mitchell swore, leaping backwards. White-faced and shaking. *Jesus,* and he shook his head, the colour slowly returning.

It was the music. He had thought the place was haunted. Thought he was entering some *fucking haunted cathedral,* and as he told us, I noticed his hands were still shaking. *God,* he said, *I've gotta get my breath back,* and he slumped down against the wall, his knees up against his chest.

It was the only lapse of his bravado.

Crouched on the floor of the verandah, not wanting to look at us looking at him, his fists curled up into two tight balls, his eyes fixed on the ground.

It was only for a moment, but for that moment none of us knew what to say.

It was Simon who broke the silence. *Here,* and he offered Mitchell his hand, helping him up, the pair of them standing together, looking at each other as they turned to follow us into the house.

It was, as Mitchell said, a dump.

But better than some of the places we've been to, I told him, and it was probably the first non-confrontational thing I had said to him all day.

Under the dim light of the few bulbs that still worked, it was clear that the place had not been inhabited for years.

The odd pieces of furniture that remained were covered, and underneath the cloth they rotted, rusty springs piercing through the upholstery. The dust was thick. Heavy, choking. Mouse droppings were underfoot. In some rooms, the boards had given way, splintering away to reveal the earth below. The beds that had mattresses sagged and creaked at the touch of a finger, stained canvas dipping low with the slightest touch.

We moved slowly from room to room. Not saying much.

We're tired, Vi said.

It's not that bad, Simon agreed.

But it was.

Later, lying on the floor with Evie in one of the three rooms we had marked out as inhabitable, I could hear Simon and Mitchell through the glass doors that separated us. Low voices just discernible in the quiet. *It's a fucking hole.*

I watched as they undressed, vague figures through the frosted glass, both tall and lean, and I leant closer, trying to hear the mutterings of their conversation. Nothing.

From the other end of the house, I could hear Vi's transistor radio. She was, no doubt, sitting up in the only bed that had seemed to be in relatively good condition, and reading.

Like her, I have difficulty going to sleep.

And I lay there, for what seemed to be hours, thinking about Mitchell crouched on the verandah, about the feel of his leg beneath my hand, and about the brief moment of his eyes, resting still, on mine.

eight

Simon telephoned the next morning. He called to tell me that Mitchell's funeral was three days away.

There was a delay, he said.

It was early. Just before he started his shift. Squeezed into the small public phone box outside the staffroom, he was wheezing slightly as he spoke. In the background, I could hear a fly buzzing around his head, flying into the glass and then back again.

I did not understand what he meant.

Because of the way he died, he tried to explain.

I opened my curtains and looked out across the sharp heat of the morning. The ocean was harsh, too bright under the fierceness of the sky. I felt nauseous again and I had to get ready for the audition.

How did he die? I asked, and I couldn't hide the frustration in my voice, despite knowing that this would only make him slower.

They had to do an autopsy, and I heard Simon draw back on

his cigarette. *I guess that's what they always do in cases like this. I don't know. Anyway, that's what his sister said.*

You called his sister?

Once again, he didn't answer my question.

That's why the funeral was delayed.

I told him I was running late, I couldn't talk and could he please tell me what had happened.

I waited.

He cleared his throat.

It was, and he stumbled for the word, *a suicide.*

And for a moment, we were both silent, neither of us sure of what to say.

Mitchell had killed himself.

Hung himself, Simon said.

I sat up slowly and pushed the sheet off me.

From above, I could hear one of them, Anton or Louise, opening a window wide, letting in whatever slight breeze drifted off the sea, and I, too, reached across the small space of my room and opened the door that leads out to the garden. Nothing. Just the still heat and the whirr of the cicadas, starting already. Early.

Did his sister know who you were?

He told me he had said he was a friend. That was all.

Please, he asked, *can you come? I don't want to go alone.*

I didn't answer him. Not straightaway. I didn't know what to say.

I could hear a bus pulling out from the depot, the groan of the engine as it shifted into first gear, and I could hear Simon leaning against the door to the booth, heavy against the glass.

And I agreed, wishing I hadn't as soon as the words were out of my mouth. Wishing I could take them back.

I'll go there with you, I said, *but I won't go to the service.*

He didn't argue.

I'll pick you up, he said. *Friday morning.*

He had to go. His shift was about to start.

Have you told Vi? I asked.

I've got to go, he said again. *Friday morning, nine o'clock,* and he hung up, leaving me with all my questions still hanging, useless, in the air.

I, too, was going to be late. I could see the clothes I had ironed hanging off the curtain railing, my diary open with the address and the time written in red, and my dinner from the night before still in the bowl next to my chair, ants swarming up the sides, thousands of them, and I watched as they carried the leftovers away, piece by piece.

It was not until I heard him, Mouse, turning on the shower, the high-pitched grate of the rusted pipes, that I actually hung up the phone and moved. With my towel and shampoo in one hand, I knocked on the bathroom door, loudly, trying to be heard above the roar of water hitting the tin bath.

What's your problem? he shouted.

I told him I was late, that I needed to have a shower quickly, that it was urgent, I had an audition. But I knew it was useless.

He started singing. Loudly. Tunelessly.

I went back into my flat, slamming the door behind me so that the whole building shuddered, the windowpanes rattling, precarious, and then still.

nine

Violetta was actively involved in the first campaigns to legalise abortion.

I remember.

A new sticker suddenly appeared on my school folder: 'Our bodies, our choices', in bold purple.

I looked at it and I looked at her, waiting for me to ask her what it meant.

I didn't want to oblige. I didn't want another long sermon, but whether I asked or not, she would explain. So I shrugged my shoulders, stared out the window and asked her what it was about.

She told me. And it all made perfect sense. So much so that I couldn't even begin to see why there was a debate.

But, nevertheless, I still spent most of the afternoon scratching that sticker off with my fingernails. Not because I disagreed, but because it didn't go with the overall colour scheme, the pictures I had cut out and painstakingly pasted into a collage.

Do you know what you said when I saw you'd taken it off? Vi asks me.

I can't remember.

My folder, my choice, and she laughs. *You were such a smart arse.*

We both smile.

As I try to help Vi collate some of her papers, she remembers the details of every struggle like she would remember family members. And, invariably, the work that we have set out to do is pushed to one side as she reminisces.

We had to be extreme, she says. *We had to take a black and white stance. Sometimes the only way you can get a message across is by ignoring the complexities, by pushing a simplistic truth as forcefully and as often as you can.*

Take this, and she holds a copy of one of those stickers up for me to see.

I had a termination once, and she looks out the window. *It was not the simple choice that we always defined it as.*

I am surprised by what she says and I want to know when, but she shakes her head.

It was a long time ago. A married man. Before your father. She turns back to the papers at our feet.

Vi wants me to have a child. It has been something she has wanted for a long time. But even more so since she became ill.

I have never told her that I did try once. With Marco. For about a year.

It was more at his instigation than through my own desire. When nothing happened, he wanted to have tests, but by then I knew that it wasn't right. That it shouldn't go on.

Vi tries to push a box of files towards the door, and I have to stop her. She is coughing and the hack from deep in her chest is fierce and rough.

When I suggested clearing out her workroom, I was surprised by the enthusiasm with which she embraced the idea. And then I realised. She did not see it as a packing up, as an ending – she saw it as a clearing of the decks to make way for the new, for her next projects. And this is the way we have approached it.

On the good days I am hopeful that this is in fact what it is, but on the days when I hear that cough again, I am fearful that we have just been fooling ourselves.

Whenever I failed to get a part, Marco would try to cheer me up.

Listen to how bad it is, and he would read out two or three of the worst lines in the script, usually so appallingly that I would have to smile.

You should be relieved, he would say. *Imagine having to suffer your way through this.* He would read a little more, unaware of how truly expressionless he could make something sound.

A pitiful opiate for the masses? I would ask.

Exactly, and he would smile.

But even when he made me laugh, it did not lessen the hurt that usually follows a rejection. The knowledge that you are, somehow, not good enough.

And that was how it was on the afternoon of my audition. I knew I was not what they were looking for. There were five of us who had been asked to read. We were all the same height, the same build and had the same colour hair, but there was only one of us who was right. And although I had hated the role, it was as I had known it would be: once I did not have it, I wanted it.

I rang work and told them I could not come in. My boyfriend was still unwell. Worse, in fact. They understood. They like to think of themselves as a supportive team.

I caught the bus home and, with my head pressed against the window, I stared out at the grit of the day. The sky was swollen. Purple. Everything was still. Not a whisper of air. Against the vinyl of the bus seat, my shirt stuck to my back. I opened the window wide, and I closed my eyes, trying to imagine how I had felt before this nausea had overtaken me.

If Marco were at home, if everything had not panned out in the way it had, he would tell me that things would change, that there would be a turn. I would be in more constant work and, what's more, I would be getting parts I wanted.

You'll see, he would say.

I promise, he would say.

And as I thought about the possibility of those words, of his familiarity, I wished I could call him.

But I knew that what I was remembering was not the way it had eventually come to be. As the years had passed, he would still try to cheer me up, but not as often and not for as long, and I would sense in the stiffness of his shoulders, in the tightness of his neck, that he had become impatient with me, and with my life.

He once told a friend that there was nothing quite so difficult as an out of work actor.

It's your self-indulgence, he had said after I had thrown a glass at him. *It's so bloody boring.*

It did not stop me.

When the bad weeks came, it was not just my work. I would barely speak, furious with him for not being able to follow me in the losses that I was traversing. I would find myself remembering the Simon Marco had never met.

I used to have such a crush on your brother, my older friends would sometimes say to me.

And they did. Everybody did.

He was himself, I would say to Marco, but I knew I did not do justice to what my brother had once been.

He was shy, gentle.

Open.

And then he had retreated.

I don't know how he can bear it, I would say, thinking of him living with Vi, never falling in love, driving buses all day.

Maybe he's happy, and Marco would barely look up from the book he was reading. *Maybe it's just you who can't bear the thought of his life. Maybe it's simply your expectations that have been disappointed.*

Not surprisingly, his words did little to arrest the downward spiral that I had carved out for myself, that I was determined to complete. I would force myself to go back to that night all those years ago at Candelo, and I would see things that I hadn't really seen because I hadn't been there at the time.

And then there was Evie.

Clutching her joke book, her legs in the arms of her T-shirt, and her pants worn on her arms.

Why did the germ cross the microscope?

This is how I remember her.

Still.

Because he wanted to get to the other slide.

Marco would tell me that I should stop moping. That I should get on with things. That it did not do anyone any good to lie around. To wallow. And (most important of all) that there were countless people out there a lot worse off than me.

I could see that he did not intend to be harsh, that he was simply trying to help.

Are you all right? he would ask later, and as he leant forward to kiss me, I would find myself pulling away and I would see the hurt in his eyes.

It was not that he did not care. It was just that his way was not my way.

There's no point to this, he would say. *You just have to get on.*

Because that is what he had done. He had got on.

Look at your life, he would say, and I would know that he was holding his own up for comparison.

He had been a builder. He had run away from an alcoholic father and started work when he was fifteen. At twenty he took himself back to school and then on to university, studying at night and working during the day. His days and his evenings were full. He now works in industrial relations, and his climb up the union ladder has not only been rapid, it is also far from over.

My life did not make sense to him. It never would. He secretly felt that my moods came from too little to do. He would tell me it was up to me. He would try to offer practical advice. Ways of getting out of the rut, possible career changes, and then, of course, there was the baby option.

Why not? he asked.

And as he moved to kiss me again, I would close my eyes, wanting to pull away, wanting to turn my head, but not wanting to see that hurt in his eyes.

So, we tried, despite the fact my heart was never in it.

And as I sat on the bus, I looked down at my stomach. There was no sign, no visible indicator, no evidence of what I knew was there.

But it was there. And as I let the realisation seep in, I wished I knew what to do.

ten

In the dark of that first night, I woke and I did not know where I was.

Candelo.

I whispered the word to myself. Trying it. Rolling each syllable out, smooth and round.

Next to me, Evie slept. Curled up on the mattress, covered by a sheet, the blanket kicked down to her feet, her thumb in her mouth.

Outside I could hear the branches scratching against the window, rattling against the glass with each faint stirring of the breeze. The shadows on the wall drifted, floating backwards, forwards. From the room next door I could hear one of them snoring. Mitchell, or Simon. Each intake of breath. Each exhalation.

I could not sleep.

The floor was gritty beneath my feet. Years of dust and dirt, leaves that had drifted in through cracks beneath doors, holes in floorboards, twigs, sticks, cockroaches that darted into corners and a door that creaked as I opened it, the milky light of the moon spilling out across the corridor, crisscrossed by the branches tap-tapping against the window.

I looked from one end of the hall to the other, the darkness on either side of me, the long worn runner only just visible as I made my way, quietly, carefully, towards the thin strip of yellow light under Vi's door, letting myself in without knocking.

Already her room looked like her room. Her papers laid out on her desk, the typewriter out of its case, her dresses hung in the cupboard, her transistor radio on, late-night classics in the stillness of the night.

Who lived here? I asked her.

She put her book down, the spine bent and worn, and took her glasses off.

Some friends of some friends of some friends, and she pulled back the sheet on the other side of her bed, moving over to make space for me.

Used to my insomnia, she did not question the fact that I was up at this hour.

Why did they leave?

She shrugged her shoulders. *Who knows? The manager takes care of everything now and he has his own house.* She smelt of soap and, beneath that, the faint trace of cigarettes and sweet cheap perfume.

I sat on the bed next to her and looked at what she was reading. *Women and Power.* I rolled my eyes, and asked her if she was going to be working the whole time we were here.

This isn't work, she said.

From next to her bed I could hear the faint tick of her

father's watch. I picked it up and held it between the palms of my hands, the glass cold on my skin. He left it to her when he died. Large and old-fashioned, it has always looked out of place on her thin wrists. But it is precious to her. She loved her father. He brought her up. A Polish emigrant who worked hard to make sure she had the advantages he never had.

I held it to my ear and listened to its steady tick.

Why did he have to come? I asked and I nodded my head in the direction of Mitchell and Simon's room.

She told me she thought I had got over that.

I told her I hadn't, but she could see from the look on my face that I was just bored, that I was just trying it on.

The metal awning over the window of her room lifted in the breeze. A slow, mournful whine in the quiet.

What happened to his family?

She looked at me, and as she pushed her glasses back up onto the bridge of her nose, I could see she was weighing up how much to tell me. *A lot of people find it exceptionally difficult to make ends meet. In Mitchell's case, there were a lot of problems that made it impossible for him to be at home for long stretches at a time.*

It was, as I had expected, a totally unsatisfying response.

She put on her glasses and picked up her book again.

I leant over her shoulder: *Gender inequity persists and will continue to persist.* My mouth was pursed and my face was serious. *You really find this interesting?* I asked, and I yawned.

She reached for the watch, now fastened on my wrist.

Can I wear it? I asked. *Just tonight?*

She shook her head.

Her father had been a doctor in Poland. He was an orderly when he came out here. Cleaning floors, making beds. *Too scared to fight. Too scared to change things,* Vi once told me.

He worked in the one hospital for over twenty years. Night shifts. Day shifts. Whatever was offered to him, until finally, at sixty-five, he retired.

He came home that night, sat in his armchair, put his head in his hands and wept, Vi said.

And that was how he stayed. For the next three months. Until the day he died.

She told me it was time I went to bed.

I tried to argue, but she took the watch off my wrist and shooed me away with her other hand.

No more talking, she said. *You either sleep here or you go back to your own room.*

I closed her door gently and in the darkness of that hall I listened to each sound of that house. Each shift, each creak, each groan, each rustle of each leaf, each insect darting along each skirting board, and the slow click of another door, opening and closing.

Pressed against the wall, I watched him. Mitchell.

He was in his underpants and T-shirt, the gap between the two revealing the sharp line of his hip bones. He was looking at me looking at him. Seeing me, but not seeing me. Eyes open, but not awake. Walking towards me but not walking towards me.

Mitchell, I hissed.

He didn't turn his head.

I reached for him and then I stopped. I had heard about

sleepwalking. Stories of people who walked miles, trying to find their way home, crossing cities, rivers, even state borders.

Vi, I whispered, opening her door just a few inches, careful not to let too much light spill out, careful not to wake him.

She looked at me impatiently.

It's Mitchell. As I spoke the words, she was up immediately, anxious that something was wrong, wrapping her cardigan around her shoulders as she followed me out to the hall.

See, and I pointed to where he stood, rocking slightly, from foot to foot, down near the entrance to the kitchen.

She told me to get back to bed, but I stayed where I was, watching her as she took his arm and guided him, slowly back up that corridor towards the open bedroom door, her hand resting gently on his forearm.

The door creaked as she opened it a little more and he started.

Can't go in there, he told her as she tried to lead him back in, and she jumped at the boom of his voice. *Spiders,* and he leant forward, serious, intent. *Thousands of them.*

As I started to giggle, she turned around and glared at me.

It's okay, she told him, and she was stroking his arm awkwardly.

I listened as she pulled back the sheets for him, as she opened their window a little wider, as she came down the hall towards me. He stayed quiet.

He's all right, she said.

Opening the door to our room, I could see Evie, there on the floor in the moonlight. The blanket still at her feet, her thumb still in her mouth, the slight flicker of her eyelashes as she dreamt.

I lay down on the mattress next to hers and I wondered whether Mitchell did this every night. Whether he got up and tried to find his way back to somewhere. Or whether it had just been a one-off. The strangeness of this place. The strangeness of us.

eleven

Vi rings me often, but never about anything important. She calls to tell me about a film she saw the night before, an article she read in the paper, a distant friend who has found out she has cancer.

I ring her for similar reasons.

Nothing of significance.

Neither of us ever really listening to each other, one of us ending the conversation abruptly, suddenly bored with it, only to call the other back a few hours later.

Every so often it irritates me.

I wonder why we bother.

But I do not stop. It is like a reflex action. A blank moment in either of our days and we pick up a telephone and dial each other's number. So much so that if a significant amount of time passes without us speaking to each other, I become anxious, distracted, aware that there is something important missing, out of place, but not quite able to pinpoint it. And then I remember. I haven't spoken to Vi.

Mari, on the other hand, never calls me.

And that is why when I came home from the audition and heard her message on the machine, my immediate reaction was one of alarm.

Mari and my mother met seven years ago.

On their five-year anniversary, Mari organised a party. Lunch in Vi's garden for thirty of their closest friends. She cooked for weeks, an extraordinary Italian feast, crowned by a magnificent almond cake, three layers high and covered with crystallised violets.

Standing under the crepe myrtle, Mari gave a speech. She told the story of their first meeting. It was a story I had heard before.

It all began, and she tinkled her glass for full attention, *in a women's refuge.*

I looked across at my mother, expecting her to be uncomfortable with this public show of affection, and I was surprised. She was sitting at the end of the table with her chin resting in her hands. Her cigarette burned untouched in an ashtray by her side.

Her dark eyes were focused on Mari and she was smiling, just slightly, with a shyness I had never seen before.

I looked away, quickly.

Through the glass doors, I could see that the kitchen table was piled high with gifts and I wished I had thought of bringing something. I felt ashamed for not having recognised the occasion for what it was.

She was, I think, the only woman I had ever seen in that place with such ridiculously high heels.

Everyone laughed. Vi loudest of all, cigarette-husky and deep.

But what made them even more ridiculous was the fact that we were all there to paint the place.

Vi picked up her cigarette and waved her arm in the air. *It was the only way I could reach anything,* she called out to shouts of laughter.

I could see Simon on the other side of the garden, sitting on his own with his plate balanced on his lap, the only man in a sea of women, eyes fixed on the ground.

I remember, and Mari smiled at my mother, *watching her balancing on that ladder, proselytising about the superiority of a pastel wall compared to the brilliant yellow the women had chosen, and thinking that she was truly something else. When she actually managed to convert the entire committee into choosing pale pink for the bedrooms, I knew I had met a force to be reckoned with.*

Vi clapped her hands and called out, but Mari continued: *Five years later and I still have no hesitation in calling her extraordinary, although I am thankful to say that the taste for pink has mellowed somewhat.* She raised her glass, and I watched as they all lifted their glasses in the air. *To five wonderful years.*

It was difficult to believe it had been that long.

I remembered when I had first met Mari and it seemed so recent. She had been sitting in the garden, wrapped in Vi's dressing-gown and reading the paper.

We had introduced ourselves.

I had been awkward.

She was unperturbed.

A week later, Simon had told me she was actually living there.

As in living with each other? I had asked.

He had simply shrugged his shoulders.

I watched as they all called for Vi to respond. *Speech,* they shouted, and she eventually stood up, feigning reluctance as she took her place next to Mari under the thick mass of lilac flowers.

Even in her heels, she only came up to Mari's shoulders. Her black curls had just started to grey and I noticed for the first time that she was looking old, her olive skin pallid in the sun, her cheekbones sunken.

She produced a thick wad of notes to a loud chorus of boos. *Of course, I have something prepared,* and she smiled as she pushed her glasses back up to the bridge of her nose. *In fact, I wanted to use this occasion to speak about recent cuts to spending on women's health,* and she looked around the garden at the mass of amazed faces.

And there was, for one moment, a stunned silence.

It was hard to believe she could be serious.

But what was worse was that it was possible.

And she laughed.

I had you there, she said, raising her glass of red wine.

And the relief was instantaneous.

Thank you, she said and she took Mari's hand, holding it in her own for an instant, so brief it may not have happened.

She took her glasses off and put her papers down on the table. *All of you,* and she blew a kiss, her arms outstretched. *You are good friends,* and she looked down.

It was one of the few times I had seen my mother at a loss for something to say.

When I helped Mari wash the dishes later that afternoon, she told me she was glad I had come.

Of course I'd be here, I had said, surprised by her words.

Red wine and lazy afternoon sun had relaxed her. She put the tea towel down and rested an arm around my shoulder.

We've never really become friends, have we? she asked.

I did not know what to say. I laughed and moved away. I told her she was being silly. *Too much to drink,* I said.

But she was right. Mari and I have never really become friends. It is not that I do not like her. We have just kept our distance. But lately, I have tried harder. I am glad she is there. She loves my mother and she looks after her, and these things should not be taken lightly.

When I heard her message on my machine, I called her back straightaway.

She did not spend long asking me how I was, what I had been up to, before telling me she had called because she was worried about Simon.

From my window, I could see a storm was coming in, rolling in across the dark metallic grey of the sea.

Anton's washing was still on the line, flapping against the blackening sky. It would rain soon. Any minute. Heavy drops on the parched patches of grass that struggled to survive against the weeds.

I twirled the cord tight around my finger and watched the blood drain out, white.

Why? I asked her.

Unlike the rest of our family, Mari is direct. She had seen Mitchell's obituary. Simon had clipped it from the paper. She had tried to talk to him but he had told her little more than he had told me.

You'll go with him? she asked me.

The first of the rain had started to fall and I watched as Anton unpegged each piece of clothing, bundling them into his arms before they flew wild across the garden and out to sea. I could hear the windows upstairs straining against the sashes and I remembered. Lying in bed with him and hearing the crash. The entire frame ripped off its hinges and floating out, still, for an instant, before it shattered, a thousand pieces on the rocky path below.

I didn't want to talk to your mother about it, Mari said.

And I was surprised. Because she believes in confronting, in tackling, head on.

It would only upset her.

But I wanted to make sure you would look after him. Check that he doesn't do anything stupid.

I told her I had already promised Simon I would go. I didn't know if I would actually go to the service, but I would drive out there with him.

Thank you, she said.

And as I hung up, I remembered, way out, in the stillness of the ocean, Anton swimming from one point to the other. Swimming alongside me. Crossing the bay for the first time. Pulling himself up onto the rocks on the north end, the moss spongy beneath our feet, purple, blue and green plants sparkling as the water lapped over them. Telling me that he had never done this before, and I wasn't sure what it was that he was referring to. Kissing? Kissing someone other than Louise? Or swimming from one end to the other? Telling me he shouldn't be doing this. But not stopping. And not knowing why he was saying what he was saying because I did not, not for one instant, think of either of them. Louise or Marco. Showing him a starfish. Right there, pressed against the side of a rock and him not looking, just telling me he should get back, but kissing me again. And again.

And I had thought, this is it. This is what I wanted. And I have it, right here, right now, perfect for this instant.

I tapped on my window. I knocked on the glass. I forced it open against the onslaught of wind, and I called out to him.

Anton, my voice ringing out across the garden.

He turned and he looked at me. The rain streaking down, heavy, hot, and the washing bundled under his arms.

He glanced upstairs, and then back at me, and I saw the fear on his face.

Anton, I called again, determined now to finish what I had started.

And as he ran over to my window, he was shaking his head. *She's upstairs,* he was saying. *She's upstairs.*

I told him I needed to talk to him.

Please, I said.

And I opened my front door and waited for him to come in.

twelve

My friend Lizzie has just fallen in love.

After six years on her own, she is excited and wants to talk of nothing else. It is all too good to believe.

She tells me she met him at a Buddhist meditation retreat. Nine days of silence and stolen glances across a cold draughty hall. Nine days of wondering.

And on the tenth?

We snuck out to the garden without a word, she says.

At first I am surprised, even shocked, but then I am not.

Lizzie is an academic. She lectures in philosophy. Reserved and serious, she went straight from school to university and has never left. We met in first year, drinking in the bar. After two or three beers, Lizzie would become loud and sociable and I would become progressively more introverted, both of us soon realising our differences were not as marked as we had originally thought.

She tells me she has put her doctorate to one side. She has stopped meditating and stopped going to yoga.

I don't think I've ever felt like this before, she says, and she asks me for the third time what kind of tea I want.

Her lounge room is cool and calm. All white, with little sign of any inhabitation; I usually feel myself relax when I am at her house. But this time I am agitated. We have met because I need to talk to her. I want to tell her of the decision I have had to make. I want her reassurance, but glowing with her own excitement, I know I will have to wait. I will have to listen.

How many times have you been in love? she asks me.

I tell her I don't know. Maybe three.

Marco? she asks.

Yes, Marco.

Anton? She is cautious as she mentions his name.

Perhaps.

And?

Mitchell, I tell her, surprising myself as I say his name out loud.

She, too, is surprised. But only because she has never heard me speak of him.

I was only fourteen, I say, and I am not looking at her. I am wishing I had never spoken. *I lost my virginity to him,* I tell her, and to my horror, I am blushing.

This is what happens. You find you are revealing an intimacy, telling it as a story, and suddenly you wish you weren't. It is more painful than you have let yourself realise. It is something that should not be spoken out loud. At least, not in that way.

I am staring at the neat pile of books on her desk, hoping she will not ask me to go on, *to tell*, because I do not want to speak of it.

I do not know what Mitchell thought of us, of our family. He never said, and I can only guess at his bemusement.

My friends like hearing my childhood stories. We were an oddity. It seemed that no one else had divorced parents, no one else had a mother who worked, no one else ate ratatouille, and I certainly didn't know of anyone else who had gone to a nudist commune for their summer holidays (this was the year before we went away with Mitchell).

At that time this country was deeply conservative. Vi would argue passionately that it still is and I would probably agree with her, but I would still maintain that it is less so now than it was then.

Our difference was, no doubt, accentuated by the suburb in which we lived and the schools to which we were sent. Despite Vi's staunch beliefs, after she and Bernard had separated, we stayed in the well-heeled middle-class area in which we had grown up, and both Simon and I went to a very expensive private high school (coeducational but private nonetheless).

Most of my friends were envious. I was allowed to smoke dope, drink alcohol and sleep with boys. Not only was I allowed to, but I was allowed to do it at home.

Their parents did not approve.

I remember when a friend of mine once stayed the night. Her mother picked her up the next morning. Vi pointed the way to my bedroom. We were not expecting her and she opened the door to find us smoking a joint.

She complained to Vi.

She complained to my father.

She finally gave up on them and complained to the school.

Vi refused to go and discuss the matter with the headmaster. She didn't see that there was a problem at all. She also didn't see that it was any of their business. Bernard promised he would come in for an appointment, but after his secretary postponed it for him three times in a row, they eventually gave up.

But it was not just the liberty we had that was unusual. There was also the manner in which Vi liked to run the household, the procedures aimed at creating a pretence of democracy.

On our first morning at Candelo, Mitchell had to endure a house meeting.

Because it was breakfast there was no red wine and stale cheese. There was, instead, black coffee and rye bread toasted to a crisp.

Mitchell sat at one end of the table, his hair uncombed, a slight stubble on his face, his dark eyes sleepy. He hadn't wanted to get up. I had heard Simon trying to wake him and I had heard Mitchell complaining.

It's a house meeting, Simon had explained.

A what? Mitchell had asked.

I was at the door to their room, hand poised, ready to knock, ready to tell them to hurry up.

Vi likes to talk about things. I saw Simon roll his eyes and I was surprised. He was always the most patient when it came to Vi's meetings.

He looked up and noticed I was there. *You could've knocked,* he told me, irritated by the fact that I had just come in.

I ignored him. *She wants to tell us what we have to do,* I said, and as I explained this to Mitchell, I was about to add that I had seen him. Last night. Sleepwalking. But I changed my mind. *She's waiting,* I said, and because Simon was still glaring at me, I left them both, closing the door loudly behind me.

Vi gave Mitchell another explanation. She told him that she believed in a fair and open decision-making process. In treating young people as adults. In participation.

We like to hold these meetings so that everyone has a say.

Mitchell nodded, his eyes wide, trying not to look too stunned by the concept.

Obviously, I have certain expectations, and she rolled herself the first cigarette for the day, her thin fingers moving rapidly across the paper. *I need to get some work finished, and when I'm doing that I like to be left alone. I'm also very tired from yesterday's drive and there's a lot to be done around the place.* She drew back sharply on the cigarette and I saw her face relax with the first rush of nicotine.

She looked at Mitchell and smiled. *And you?*

He had no idea what she meant.

Your expectations, I told him, my eyebrows raised. *You know, breakfast in bed, that kind of stuff.*

Vi suggested we divide up the chores democratically. When we failed to volunteer for anything, she poured herself another coffee and drew up a roster.

Mitchell and I had the lounge and the bathroom.

Simon, the kitchen.

And this afternoon, we need to go into town and get some food, she said, ashing onto her plate.

I can do that, Mitchell offered.

We were surprised.

If you're busy.

They looked at each other, momentarily.

I could see that Vi didn't want to ask.

He reached across for the matches. *I got my licence last month,* and the match flared, almost singeing his fringe. *Up to you,* he added, scraping the tip, black lines, on the edge of the table.

Vi picked up the plates. *We'll see,* she said and, putting them down in the same spot from which she had taken them, she left us to get to work.

I was the one who challenged him.

Outside the door to his and Simon's room, I told him I didn't believe he had a licence.

Whatever, he shrugged his shoulders.

Show me, I demanded.

He was putting on his jeans, standing in a clear shaft of light at the foot of his bed. I hadn't meant to look, but I had put my head around the door and there he was, his clothes scattered at his feet, his jeans half on, his shirt flung across the pillow.

I guess you've had a look for yourself.

And to my fury, I blushed, turning my back on him quickly, hoping he hadn't seen.

thirteen

Evie was a mistake.

None of us has ever said this out loud, but it is not difficult to surmise.

When I visit Vi now, she often wants to talk of her. After years of silence, it is hard to get used to this new mentioning of her name. But since my mother was told she has emphysema, a lot has changed.

She no longer smokes. The doctors told her she has a choice. Cigarettes or death, and she has stopped, but not without wavering. She is out for dinner and she reaches for a packet on the table near her.

Mari cannot believe it. *Even if you don't mind dying, think of me,* she says. *Think of how I would be without you.*

She also no longer works. Not in the way she used to. She has been told to rest. Until her blood pressure is lowered.

This, too, is not easy for her.

When I first used to visit her, Mari would always make her stay on the couch, a pile of books by her side. Novels.

My mother has never read a novel in her life.

And because Mari was terrified of Vi getting a chest infection, she would make an endless series of lemon and honey drinks that sat, barely sipped, by my mother's side.

I can't bear them, she would confess to me. *All that garlic.*

She would ask me to throw them down the sink while Mari was not looking. *It's ridiculous,* she would say. *I'm not even sick.*

But on the bad days her cough is raw and the dark circles under her eyes are deep.

She was a beautiful child, she tells me and I know she is talking of Evie. *You were all beautiful,* she adds, *although you were the most trouble of all.*

And I was. Like my mother, I was always the agitator. Twice suspended for being argumentative.

But I was secretly proud of you, she confesses and she wheezes slightly as she laughs.

Sometimes I wonder what would have become of her, and she looks out the window.

I do not know what to say. I have also wondered this. What she would have been like. Whether we would have been close.

I can't help myself, and she coughs again, a cough fierce enough to shake her whole body.

She asks me to bring her papers in to her, the next bundle to sort, and I do. Because, unlike Mari, I think that not working is more stressful for my mother than working. But when I give them to her, she wants to talk of Evie again.

She was stubborn too. Not compliant like Simon.

She was. I remember. Even with the nine years between us (eleven between her and Simon), we were already fighting.

This age difference was one of the reasons why I know she was a mistake. The gap was too large. The other was my father.

When Vi found out she was pregnant, he confessed. He had been seeing someone else. A couple of people actually. For several years.

I was only eight, but I remember it clearly. I remember their fights. Sometimes they would last all night. Both of them shouting at each other, doors slamming, waking to find one or other of them asleep in the spare bed in my room.

My father didn't want another child. He never said as much. But looking back, it is not hard to see that this was how he felt.

When he finally left, he did so without telling any of us. Not even a note. He just went off to work and did not come home, leaving everything: his clothes, his books, his records.

Vi got a letter from him two days later, telling her not to worry, and then nothing. We did not hear from him for months.

She threw all of his possessions out onto the street. Six months pregnant, tottering in her sandals, weighed down by the bundles she was carrying, refusing to stop until it was all gone. Every last thing.

Well, she said, *that's that,* and she poured herself a whisky, lit a cigarette and sat down at her desk to write an article.

When she went into labour, she went to hospital on her own. She packed her bags and called a taxi, dropping Simon and me at a friend's on the way.

Bernard did not visit her or the baby. He did not even ask after them. Years later, he tried to talk to me about it. He had just done a group therapy weekend and rang me as soon as he got home. He wanted to apologise. For being such an absent father. An appalling father. He needed to know that I forgave him. And as he talked to me, he started to cry.

I was speechless.

Don't, I finally managed to say.

He told me he understood if I did not want to talk. But he needed to tell me he was sorry.

We never mentioned it again.

I assume he made the same call to Simon, and I can only guess that Simon would have responded a little more sympathetically than I had. He, too, would have been uncomfortable with Bernard's outburst, but at the least, he would have listened without judging.

Sometimes when I am visiting Vi, when I am sitting with her on the couch, or sorting her papers, Simon comes home. He stands, bulky in the doorway, and for a moment he does not know whether to come in or whether to go straight to his room.

Hi, he says, and he seems about to take a step towards us, but then he changes his mind.

I can see the hesitation on his face and I know why he falters.

He wonders whether we have been talking about Evie again.

He scratches his hand nervously and he turns to the stairs, and I know he must fear the places to which our talk could lead.

To Candelo.

To Mitchell.

And to the funeral that neither of us has mentioned since our return.

fourteen

Vi never told us what she knew about Mitchell. What was in the files. The few scraps of information she gave us, coupled with the little that he said, comprised the sum total of all I knew.

He was sixteen. He had been to four foster homes. He had never finished school. He sleepwalked. His family was poor. He wanted to surf. And he wanted to be in a band.

With the broom handle in one hand, he winked at Evie and started to sing. Badly. She wrinkled up her nose and blocked her ears.

You sound terrible, she told him.

He looked at us. Even Simon shook his head in acknowledgement. *Maybe you could learn an instrument,* he suggested.

Or use it to sweep, and I pointed at the broom handle, now clutched in his hands like a guitar.

He followed me into the lounge room, still singing, leaving Simon and Evie in the kitchen.

The room was even more of a mess in daylight, the curtains hanging by two or three hooks, the fabric torn and soiled, the chairs covered in sheets thick with dust, the paint peeling off the walls and the fireplace piled high with rubbish.

With my sleeve, I rubbed a circle in the dirt that coated the window and looked out over the garden, the fruit trees, the remains of an old well now choked with weeds, and the cypress trees marking the border between what had once been carefully cultivated and what lay beyond. In the distance, I could see the miles of rolling paddocks, not smooth, but punctuated by boulders, lichen-covered and erupting out of the earth, the stark silhouettes of streaky gums, and beyond that the grey-blue of the mountains, the snow country.

It was the stillness that was strange. I forced the window up. Nothing. Just the soft rush of the wind across the grass.

And I leant out and listened.

Can you hear? I asked Mitchell.

The quiet?

And we both stayed there, our elbows resting on the sill, not wanting to move, not wanting to break the silence.

But it didn't last. From across the courtyard, Vi began to type, the keys clattering as she wrote, followed by a long pause before she started again. In the stillness of the morning, the sound was clear, carrying through the French doors which were open wide to let in the light.

What's she doing? Mitchell asked. He lifted one of the dust sheets gingerly, uncertain as to what he would find beneath it.

I told him she was writing a paper.

What about?

I didn't know. *Welfare, domestic violence, youth crime.* I shrugged my shoulders.

What for?

And I couldn't answer him. *It's what she does.*

He whipped another sheet off a chair, this time with a flourish, the dust floating high and then falling.

Ever been to jail? I asked him, not sure how he would react but wanting to show him that he couldn't intimidate me. No matter what he said.

He lit a Winfield and sat on the window ledge.

What do you reckon?

I told him I thought he was too young.

I've been around. He grinned again, white teeth in a brown face. In the brightness of the light, I could see the scar on his knuckle more clearly. Smooth and white across his finger.

So why don't you live with your family? I asked.

He flicked the ash onto the floor.

Who says I don't?

Well, what are you doing with us?

Fucked if I know.

I was smiling before I could stop myself.

He offered me a cigarette.

Not wanting to tell him I didn't smoke, I took one. He lit it for me, leaning close, forcing me to step back.

I must have gone purple with trying not to choke, the smoke billowing out from my mouth, my nose, my ears, until I was coughing and spluttering in front of him.

He laughed.

This is how you do it, and he drew back, slowly, holding it in, holding it in, finally letting out a series of perfect smoke rings.

I was dizzy. Nauseous and reeling. But I persisted.

So where do you live? I asked him, in between sporadic fits of coughing.

Depends, and he butted out his cigarette, flicking it across the verandah. *Sometimes with foster parents. Sometimes in a home. Sometimes on me own.*

I started sweeping. My mouth tasted dry and foul, and I was concentrating on not being sick. He still hadn't moved. Leaning against the window frame, his back warm in the sun, watching me.

You know, and his voice was slow and lazy, *you've got pretty good legs. Nice tan. Not bad.*

And despite the fact that I was secretly pleased by what he had said, I glared at him.

You know, I said. *Your dick isn't bad either. Pity you wear it on your shoulders.*

He ignored me.

He looked out again at the sharp clarity of the sky above the bleached grass before slowly letting himself down from the window ledge, his gaze still fixed somewhere out beyond the garden.

I kicked the dustpan and broom towards him.

Reckon we should get this done and get down to the beach, he said. But he didn't move from where he was, standing there, staring out the window, seemingly mesmerised by what lay beyond. Miles of space. An emptiness he had probably never seen before.

I turned my back to him and went on with the sweeping. And because I was looking down, I didn't see. I just heard.

His sudden shout, loud and clear, legs disappearing over the sill as I turned around and dropped the broom, clattering at my feet. Scrambling over the verandah wall, running fast across the garden, long thick grass, towards her, Evie.

She liked to pretend she was pregnant.

I remember.

She would stuff clothes, cushions up her shirt and walk around like that all day, careful of her baby.

That was how I saw her, her pillows supported with one hand, a long stick in the other, the red of her shirt startling against the golden grass and cobalt sky. And as he hurtled towards her, she dropped everything, her mouth in a wide scream as he scooped her up in his arms. So fast it was still. Just the brilliance of those colours. That is how I see it all.

Still.

Just that image.

No sound at first. And then slowly, the breeze in the cypresses, the slap of Mitchell's thongs on the stairs as he carried her up towards us, Simon and me. And Evie's scream.

It was a snake.

I still don't understand how he had managed to see it from the house. But he had. Thick and oily, rearing up towards her, while she prodded it away with her stick. Coiled in the long grass.

And as Evie continued to scream, Vi came out from her room, papers clutched in one hand, reaching for Evie with the other; she seized her out of Mitchell's hold, and she wanted to know what had happened.

Somewhere in the distance, a crow cawed.

We all waited for the explanation.

But it wasn't him who told us.

It was Evie. Still sobbing as she described the snake.

Mitchell nodded in agreement. *So I ran and grabbed her,* he said.

And it was me who backed him up. *So quick I didn't know what was happening.*

Vi put Evie down, her glasses dropping to the ground as she bent low. I watched as she reached to pick them up, thin fingers brushing Mitchell's hand as he, too, tried to retrieve them.

I had seen the alarm on her face, the fear when she had first come out to find Mitchell holding Evie. A flicker. A moment. But enough.

She was embarrassed.

So was he.

She thanked him as he gave the glasses back to her. She thanked him again as he went back down into the garden to pick up the trail of Evie's pillows and helped her stuff them back into her shirt.

And over lunch she told him she would think about him taking the car into town to do the shopping.

And to the beach? Simon asked, his open mouth full of food as he waited for her response.

Maybe, she said. *As long as you're careful,* and she looked at Mitchell, who nodded, solemnly.

Wouldn't be anything but, he promised.

fifteen

Despite the fact that so many girls were interested in Simon, there was only ever one who went out with him.

Rebecca Hickson.

Thirteen years old, tall, blonde, captain of the softball and netball teams, popular, and always certain of getting her own way; she cornered me outside the canteen and told me that she liked my brother.

So? With my arms folded across my chest, I stared back at her.

I want to go to the Saturday dance with him.

Well, ask him, and I moved to push past her, but she put her hand firmly on mine, the chain of her charm bracelet cold against my wrist.

I have, and her stare was cool as she repeated Simon's words, as she told me that he didn't want to go.

Well, there's your answer, but as I spoke I knew there was more to this than I had at first realised, that I was not going to be allowed to leave so easily.

I want you to change his mind, and with her hand still on mine, her body still barring my way, she told me that I had until Friday. I had to get Simon to agree or she would make it known that I was the one who broke into the chemistry lab.

There was no point in telling her that I had never done anything of the kind. Rebecca Hickson's powers, coupled with my reputation, were such that she would be believed. Despite the fact that she was lying.

And knowing I had no choice, I begged Simon to go to the dance with her.

I pleaded with him.

I don't like those things, and he did not lift his gaze from the television as I told him that that wasn't the point. The point was that she would make my life hell. The point was that it was only a small sacrifice. To save his sister. To save me.

Eventually he agreed. And on Friday, at three o'clock, he told her he had changed his mind.

I remember seeing the triumph on her face, the sheer satisfaction at having got what she wanted, what she had been denied. It did not matter that Simon left her as soon as they arrived, that he spent the night sitting outside watching Michael Arnold get so drunk that he took all his clothes off and danced naked under the flagpole; all that mattered was that she had said she was going with Simon and she had.

Anton was waiting awkwardly just inside my flat, a pool of water at his feet, dark on the floorboards, seeping into the edge of the rug, and as I looked at him, I wished I hadn't asked him to come in.

I wished I didn't have to say what I had to say.

The rain was heavy now. Loud and relentless. I knew I would need to put pots out to catch the drips from all the spots in the ceiling that leaked in downpours such as this, but I would do it later.

As we stood opposite each other, uncomfortable and without words, I remembered my determination in pursuing him and I could not help but wonder whether I deserved the situation in which I had found myself.

Because I had been determined.

Each morning, I would wake early, and extricate myself, limb by limb, from the heaviness of Marco's body.

Don't go, and, half asleep, he would try to pull me back down into the tight grip of his arms.

But I was gone.

Bare feet on bare boards, bathers still damp from the day before, I would close the door behind me and step out into the freshness of the day, the brilliance of the blue sky, blue sea and the first of the morning glory, opening purple and full to the sun.

The stairs that lead down to the beach are cracked and the path they make is overgrown. Thick, glossy mirror bush blocks out the light; dark, secret caves beneath their branches. I always stand at the top, still for a moment, and look out to the ocean. On the days when it is flat, I swim the bay; when it is rough, with king tides that sweep up to the rocks below the cliff path, I go to the pool.

And this was how we got to know each other.

I would find myself waiting, there at the top of the stairs, until I heard him coming up behind me. Setting it all in place, knowing what I wanted right from the start. Manoeuvring, piece by piece, until it was there in front of me. Anton smiling as he found me each morning waiting in the same spot, flicking me with his towel as he came down the stairs to stand next to me, asking me what it was going to be: *The pool or the sea for you and me?*

It was only later that I marvelled at how I failed to think of the others, at how determined I was, and when I do that, I remember Rebecca Hickson's face, and I feel ashamed. I look at myself in the mirror, and I tell myself that Anton was no Simon, dragged there against his will and refusing to participate. Despite what he would say.

But it doesn't always work.

As he stood there at my front door with his washing bundled in his arms, a peg still caught on the sleeve of a T-shirt, we could not look at each other.

I can't stay, he said, uncertain as to why I had called him in the first place, glancing nervously up to the ceiling, up to where Louise was waiting.

I know, and I moved to close the door.

I could see the rain rushing in torrents down the path and I knew that when it finally eased, the back steps would be sagging, rotting further; the rust that eats away at everything in this building would have crept a little higher into the pipes, and the paint on the walls would have peeled a little more. Slowly decaying around us.

I was pregnant.

And I felt like a fool as I told him.

It was Marco who once described Anton as *something of a used-car salesman. All charm and no substance.*

It was a comment that made me wonder how much he guessed. It was a comment that I did not want to remember as I stood there opposite him, knowing that he was going to fail me.

Are you sure? he finally asked, still not looking up at me.

I told him I was.

That it was me? The ugliness of his words crossing mine.

And as the impact of what he said hit me, I knew that if I had been another person, a third person who had walked in out of the rain and stood there at my front door, listening to this, I might have felt for him, I might have understood why he said what he said, but I didn't.

All I could do was hate him.

And wonder how I had ever fallen for him.

Don't be afraid of single-minded pursuit, Vi used to say, and she would look at me, checking to see whether I was listening.

So long as what you want is a good thing.

And I would roll my eyes at the impossibility of her addendum.

And so long as you can be certain of . . . and she would pause, for one instant, perhaps for dramatic effect, perhaps to make sure that I was paying attention.

Of what? I would ask, impatiently.

Of what you are going to find at the end.

I turned to the sink, to the pile of dirty dishes, and as I let the tap run, he reached for my hand, but I pulled away.

Please, he said, *don't tell her,* and he glanced up to the ceiling

91

again, to where the telephone rang, to where a chair scraped overhead, to where footsteps clattered across the room, to where Louise leant out the window to see where he was, to see what had happened to him.

What happens, I asked him, *if I want to go ahead, if I want to do this?*

The window slammed closed above us.

We could hear her, walking down the corridor, to the front door, and in Anton's eyes there was only fear.

But you can't, his words a whisper, her footsteps on the landing, on the stairs, as he looked at me.

I don't know what I want, I said, the tap still running as he tried to tell me he was sorry.

But it was too late.

We could hear her knocking on the door, and as he spoke to me, he also called out to her, telling her that he was coming, not knowing whether to open it and let her in, not knowing whether to leave her or to leave me.

It is not as though he behaved in a way I hadn't expected, I told Lizzie later. *I knew what he was like,* and I looked away.

I knew what he was like. But I had hoped for more.

I have to go, he said. *I am sorry,* he said. *We will talk,* he said. But his face said only one thing.

I didn't want this either. My voice was low as he opened the door to Louise, standing there in the rain, not knowing why she had been left to wait; the rain coursing down her hair, soaking into her shirt.

Telephone, she said, not looking at me, just looking at him.

I'd better run, he said, but not to either of us, to no one in particular, and as he turned to the stairs, as he disappeared from sight, she stayed where she was.

I didn't move. There against the sink, with her at the entrance to my flat.

Are you okay? she asked, and I told her I was.

Just a bit of family trouble, and, as if on cue, I knocked the answering machine, replaying Mari's message asking me to call her. I reached for the stop button, but it was too late. The message had played out.

Well, she said, *I suppose I'd better go too.*

But she waited, just for a moment, neither of us speaking, and as I watched the rain falling behind her, I wondered whether she knew.

Because it was possible we had all been lying. Not just he and I. But all of us.

To each other and to ourselves.

sixteen

When Simon was fourteen, he took up art. Life drawing, to be exact.

I remember.

He found out about it through an advertisement in the local paper and told Vi he wanted to join. Once a week she would drive him over to where the group met and pick him up again three hours later.

All housewives, I overheard Vi telling a friend, knowing she had used a term she hated because it was the only way to describe the incongruity of Simon's presence, *and him.*

I was fascinated. But not with the housewives.

You have a nude model? I asked him, looking at the charcoal drawings he brought home. Drawings of an exceptionally voluptuous woman lying back on a mound of velvet pillows. *Completely starkers?*

He was disparaging in his response. *What do you reckon?*

She had the most enormous pair of breasts I had ever seen. *So where does she undress?*

He found it difficult to comprehend the inanity of my question.

Where do you think?

I had no idea.

She doesn't get cold?

He rolled his eyes in response.

He had his drawing on the very expensive easel Bernard had bought for him in one of his sporadic attempts at being an interested father. I watched as he worked, concentrating on perfecting the curve of the hip, smudging the charcoal with his hand, stepping back, smudging again.

She doesn't get embarrassed? I asked.

He had no idea what I meant.

In front of you?

Being only twelve, I was at an age when nudity and sex were still, by and large, a mystery. Vi had, of course, explained everything to us in long and boring detail, but I could not help but feel there was something more. Something she had left out.

I had never even kissed a boy.

I didn't know about Simon; I had always presumed he was as inexperienced as I was. He was too enveloped in his own world to even contemplate the possibility of some physical connection with another.

Do you ever get embarrassed? I asked.

He looked at me. *Of course not.*

Do you ever get, you know, and I searched for the word I wanted, enjoying needling him, enjoying frustrating his endless patience, *a stiffie?*

I stared straight at him, not blinking, not giggling, despite desperately wanting to, and waited for his answer.

He blushed. Crimson.

I started laughing.

He turned his back to me, but I could see, from the shake of his shoulders, that he was laughing too. Not wanting me to know, but unable to hide it effectively.

Well, do you? I asked, knowing I was pushing it now.

He didn't turn around.

You can tell me.

There was still no response.

Just answer me.

It took a lot to make my brother crack.

And then I'll go.

He turned the radio up.

Just yes or no.

I wouldn't give up. Not until he lost it.

Tell me.

Because he drove me crazy.

And, no doubt, I did the same to him.

My father has one of Simon's drawings in his chambers. A nude that he did when he was fifteen. It hangs in a corner of the room, not readily visible to any visitor, but it is there and that, in itself, is surprising.

I like it. As an adult, I can see that it is fairly crude, but there is something jovial and energetic about this woman with her big hips, big breasts and big lips. She makes me smile. Possibly because I remember my conversations with Simon whenever I see her.

Simon still draws. But it is no longer large, overblown nudes on his easel. His pictures are small, tight portraits. Portraits of himself. He has never shown them to me, but I have seen them. Once when he came to visit, he left his book behind. I found it and I flicked through it guiltily, wishing I hadn't as soon as I had.

There was not a nude in sight.

Just Simon. Eyes averted. Looking anywhere but at himself.

She cheers me up, my father said when he came in from court and found me standing by the picture.

He kissed me on the cheek, and asked me if I was ready. I told him I was.

My father has always liked taking me out. About once a month he books an expensive restaurant, one where he is bound to bump into colleagues and clients. I think he secretly hopes I will do something slightly outrageous or bohemian, something that will enhance the eccentric image he tries to cultivate.

We had arranged this particular lunch some weeks ago. With all that was on my mind, I would have forgotten, but his secretary, Melinda, had called me at work to remind me. She was new at the job and, as Bernard said, *frighteningly efficient.*

On that day I was dressed for the office, and I'm sure my conservative skirt and shirt were a mild disappointment, although he never would have admitted as much. He told me I looked wonderful. A little tired, but wonderful.

He was in a good mood. An expansive mood. He had just won a long and difficult case that had been covered, extensively, by all the papers, and he ordered a bottle of Moët.

When I told him I only had an hour, he dismissed my concerns with a wave of his hand.

What are they going to do? Sack you?

He was right. I am, after all, his daughter.

So, he asked me, *how is the junkie business going?* This is how he likes to refer to my acting, loudly and clearly. More for the effect that he hopes it will have on those within earshot than for the value of the joke.

As I told him about the audition, how I thought I had missed out on the part, he read the menu.

I don't understand this fashion for nursery food, and he sipped his champagne. *Corn beef and mash. Hideous.*

I didn't bother continuing.

Realising he had been guilty of not listening, he patted my hand as he looked around the room. *What we need for you, my dear, is an introduction to a rich and powerful film producer. One who is embroiled in some very tricky legal business.*

I wouldn't have put it past him. And because I wanted to change the topic, I asked him about his latest girlfriend.

My father has an endless stream of affairs. He starts up with the next one while he is still with the first, so there is never a transition, a period in which he is alone. Now that I am older I can see how he does it. He is not a handsome man. But he is charming. He has limitless energy and enthusiasm.

His latest was a young lawyer called Samantha. She is only about five years older than I am. On the one occasion I have met her, she was uncomfortable. It was probably just the close proximity in our ages. But I did not warm to her.

As he told me that things had been a bit *tricky* in that

department, I knew Samantha was probably on her way out.

So who's the next one? I asked him, and he did his utmost to look offended.

Well, and he leant forward in his best conspiratorial manner, *I have had my eye on someone.*

Probably more than your eye, I said.

And he laughed.

How is your exceptionally complicated love life? he asked.

I had, in the throes of first passion and over a bottle of champagne, once told him about the entire affair. Normally I liked swapping stories with him but this time I wished I had kept silent. I told him it was over. He was staying with his girlfriend and that was that. *Not much I can do about it.*

Hence the long face? he asked.

Hence the long face, and I looked down at my plate, wanting to talk about something else.

It was not until the end of the meal that I mentioned Simon. I had been tossing up whether to tell him, uncertain as to whether it was, in fact, something he should know, and, if so, whether he would be of any use.

Being a barrister, Bernard is well trained in not revealing anything, especially when he is caught off guard. So I was surprised at his reaction, at the sudden gravity in his manner. He put his glass down on the table and lowered the tone of his voice.

How on earth did he find out? he asked me, clearly concerned.

I told him I didn't know.

And he wants to go to the funeral?

I nodded.

He sat back and rubbed his chin with his hand.

Your mother was a damn fool.

I did not know what he meant.

Taking that boy on holiday with you.

I didn't remind him that he had been distinctly uninterested in the matter at the time.

He called for the bill.

Does she know about this? he asked me.

I told him she didn't.

You can't stop him from going?

When I told him it was unlikely, he made me promise I would go with him. He made me promise I would try to keep him from doing anything foolish. *And call me,* he said, *as soon as you get back.*

Like Vi, my father does not like to talk of Evie. Her name is never mentioned. And I could only presume that his distress was due to the fact that our conversation had brought up a subject he would prefer to forget.

I reached across to take his hand. It was, I suppose, a gesture of comfort, and I was as surprised as he was by my attempt.

He squeezed my fingers in his, just for a moment, and then pulled away. The waiter had brought the bill.

seventeen

———

Vi has caught another dose of flu and is not well, but still she refuses to succumb, to see herself as ill.

I can sense her irritation as Mari takes the call each time the telephone rings. Mari turns down invitations, requests for Vi to speak, to sit on a board, to participate in a radio interview. She tells them all that she is not well and no, she doesn't know when she will be up to it.

Vi tenses.

Her voice is hoarse and cracked as she asks Mari to tell her who the caller was and what it was they wanted.

No one important, and Mari checks that Vi is warm enough, that she has everything she needs.

I try to tell Mari that perhaps this is not the best approach. My mother is someone who has always worked. She lives for her work. In all my memories of her, she is sitting behind her typewriter, chain-smoking, brow furrowed, surrounded by reports and papers.

Sometimes Simon and I would test her.

Standing outside the door to her room, Simon would giggle as I would ask her if it was okay to take some money. I wanted to buy some heroin. (This was the worst that we could think of. Although, in retrospect, telling her we wanted to join the National Party would have been far worse.)

The typewriter would not stop.

In the cloud of smoke that always surrounded her, Vi would nod her assent.

So you don't mind? I would ask again.

She would swear loudly at a key that was stuck and tell me to bring back the change.

Mari tells me that she doesn't know what choice she has. *You can see how sick she is,* she says. *I have to stop her from working.*

She is irritated with me for questioning her.

But she has nothing else, I say without thinking.

Well, I don't know what you are to her, or Simon, but I certainly hope that I am more than nothing, and she drains the pasta she is making for lunch, the steam clouding the anger on her face.

I try to placate her but I am never very good at it.

She spoons out the sauce without looking at me. *You think of something,* she says.

I don't know what to say.

Maybe if you and Simon made a little more effort we could go on some family outings, interest her in your lives. I don't know.

And I nod dumbly in agreement, but I am horrified at the thought of a family outing. It is not something that we have ever been good at, and I can't see how we would start now.

I promise her I will talk to Simon and she passes me Vi's plate with a look of scepticism.

Simon's room is dark and cluttered. He never opens the curtains and when I first go in, it is difficult to see.

His clothes are strewn across the floor and his bed is unmade. The portable television is propped up on a chair. Coffee cups and plates are piled up. His desk is covered with old newspapers and magazines.

I write him a note asking him to call me and then I'm not quite sure where to leave it. I fold it so it stands and rest it up next to the television aerial.

Sitting on his bed, I am for a moment at a loss as to what to do. I want to make it better for him. I want to help, but I do not know what he needs. On the few occasions when we have been alone since Mitchell's funeral, we have not been able to speak. Even attempts at the mundane seem impossible, and we find ourselves unable to look at each other, unable to complete sentences, turning towards the door, the window, any possible exit from the place in which we have found ourselves.

I go back down to the lounge where Vi sits on the couch, her lunch half eaten. Mari has put on a video and I am surprised to see that my mother is absorbed. But then it is not so surprising. She is disparaging about all *Hollywood rubbish* but if you actually sit her down in front of anything, she will soon be leaning forward, dark eyes intent on the screen, oblivious to any interruption.

I tell her I have to get home and she doesn't look up.

She just gives me a wave with her hand.

It is Mari who takes me to the door.

I am sorry, she says as she lets me out. *I know you've been coming around a lot. I know you've been trying.*

I tell her it is okay.

She says I look tired. Not so well myself.

And for a moment, I find myself about to speak, about to tell her everything, but as the words are forming, she says she wants me to talk to Simon. Vi has been worried about him.

I have never thought of Vi as a worrier. I have always assumed she just accepts the way we are, never really noticing or questioning our behaviour.

Obviously I have been wrong.

He has been more withdrawn than ever. She pauses and looks across the street. *Possibly she just notices it more because she's not so busy.*

Again, I find myself about to speak, but stop. I know that anything I tell her will be passed on to Vi. Instead I just let her know that I have left a message for him to call me.

And I will try him, I promise, *if he doesn't get in touch.*

She looks slightly reassured, although I know she will believe it when she sees it.

And because I can see the bus coming up the hill, I leave her quickly, telling her not to worry. But I have not managed to stop myself from feeling anxious.

As I head home, I find that I am thinking about all of us, the way we were and the way we are, and when I start thinking about us, when I start remembering, I always end up thinking of Mitchell again.

And I am, once again, appalled at what happened.

I am ashamed.

I look out at the late afternoon sky and I think that there must be something I can do. Something to right all that went wrong.

I just do not know what it is.

eighteen

I have a lot of friends. Friends I go out to dinner with, friends I meet for a drink, friends I see at parties and friends I rarely see. But there are few to whom I am close.

Lizzie is different. She does not know the people I know and I do not know the people she knows. Our lives are separate so our time together is usually just the two of us.

When I first told her about Anton, some months earlier, she didn't know what to say but I could tell she thought I was being foolish.

I asked her why she thought I always made a mess of things.

She was about to utter platitudes, she was about to tell me not to be so ridiculous, but then she caught my eye. She does not like to lie.

I guess it's all relative, she said.

Her answer irritated me. I had wanted her to tell me what was wrong with me, how I could fix myself, how I could stop lurching from disaster to disaster, and how I could fall in love and stay in love.

I asked her if she thought what I was doing was wrong.

She was uncomfortable.

Not wrong, she said, and she paused.

What? I asked.

She didn't look at me. *Maybe cowardly. That's all.*

Her words hurt.

Sitting in reception at work, feeling ill from the lunch with Bernard, I wanted to talk to her. I wanted her advice, but I was scared of her disapproval. I was scared of what I knew she would think.

Instead, I called my friend Sabine. I do not know her well, but I know her well enough to know she is not like Lizzie. Not at all.

She told me she was bored. Sick of her life. That her father had bought her a ticket to Africa and that I should go with her. There was no point in telling her I had no money.

God, me too, she would have said. *It's a drag.*

I told her I had to go. I was at work. I would talk to her later.

I left a message for my friend Matthew. We had talked about doing voice classes together. I asked him to call me, I said I wanted to book, and as I was about to hang up, I told him that I also wanted to talk. I needed his advice. But as I spoke those words, I knew I wouldn't ask him if he did call. I would not tell him.

I picked up my address book and I flicked through the names. Pages and pages of them, addresses scribbled out, new numbers replacing old, new friends replacing those with whom I had lost touch or with whom I had fallen out.

I started drawing up a list. Those who would tell me that I should go ahead, that I could have a baby, and those who would tell me no. And I was, for a moment, carried away with the idea that this was not so stupid. That this was as good a way as any of coming to a decision.

But then I saw myself. Reflected in the glass reception doors. And I looked ridiculous. With my book open in front of me, my pencil in one hand, and my hair a mess about my face.

This was no way to tell right from wrong. This was no way to know.

I screwed up the piece of paper, and as I threw it in the bin, I called Simon and left a message for him. I told him we needed to meet. After work. We needed to talk. It was important.

We were bored. The three of us, Mitchell, Simon and I.

We watched the flies cluster on the few scraps of wrinkled tomato left from lunch, the wilted lettuce, the smear of butter across the plates, but we did not move to put anything away.

Reckon she'll give us the car? Mitchell asked.

Don't know, and Simon stretched, lazily.

Reckon we should go and ask her now? and he looked at each of us, wanting our opinion.

We could hear her typewriter. She had only just started again. It was not a good time to interrupt her.

Better to wait, Simon said.

Just for a while, I told him.

He drummed the tabletop with his fingertips. He picked up a glass. He put it down. *About an hour, you reckon?*

About an hour, we told him. In unison.

Outside it was hot. Midday heat that burnt the grass white, flat and colourless.

With his back on the concrete, Mitchell lay on top of the low wall that bordered the verandah, his shirt off, letting the sun soak into the smooth brown of his chest. With his arms behind his head, I could see the curls of underarm hair, golden in the light.

Ever had a girlfriend? he asked Simon, and I saw Simon shake his head.

Me neither, not a proper one, and I watched as Mitchell swung himself up, as he leant against the verandah post, his body outlined by the bright blue of the sky.

But jeez, I'd like one, and I watched him stretch; I watched his back as he stared out across the garden. *Not just someone to, you know,* and as he turned, as he looked at me, I saw Simon look down, tearing a strip of rubber off his thong, staring at his feet.

What about you? and it was me he was asking this time, and I was good at the bravado, good at the game.

A girlfriend? and I raised my eyebrows as Mitchell looked at me. *Boyfriends* ... and I shrugged my shoulders to signify the countless thousands I'd had.

But Mitchell had turned away, away from both of us.

I'd like to be in love, he said, but not to us. To no one in particular.

And I picked a cobweb, sticky and fine, off my leg and rolled it into a tight ball between my fingers.

I'd like to have kids, he said. *You know. Kids and a wife.*

Simon pulled himself up slowly from where he had been

sitting. He did not look at me and he did not look at Mitchell.

Don't know when it'll happen, but, and Mitchell turned slowly to where we both were, there behind him, to me watching him and to Simon looking down at the ground, one hand on the doorhandle, one foot inside, one still outside.

He had been about to go back inside. To disappear, without a word. But as Mitchell had turned, he had stopped.

I could hear a fly buzzing near my ear, but I did not move, and in the silence that had descended, I thought I could also hear it again, the low rush of the wind coming down from off the mountains, sweeping across the paddocks.

Mitchell's voice broke the quiet. *So, you reckon an hour's up?*

Simon looked at his watch. *No,* he said.

Let's ask her anyway, and Mitchell pointed out towards the horizon, towards where he imagined the beach was. *Let's go. Take your board,* and with his arms outstretched, he pretended to surf, the excitement sparking in his eyes. *Reckon she'll say yes?*

With one hand still on the doorhandle, Simon looked at Mitchell. They smiled at each other in a moment that I later knew excluded me.

Maybe, he said.

And as the door slammed shut behind him, as he went to ask Vi for the keys, Mitchell started humming surf tunes. Badly.

nineteen

Because he has been a bus driver for such a long time, Simon can get whatever shifts he wants. Although you earn more on nights or weekends, he usually gives up his highly valued hours to anyone who asks him, the needs of others always taking precedence over his own.

Sometimes I catch one of his buses home. I sit on the seat behind him and we talk awkwardly in between stops. The buses he drives are always crowded. He cannot bear to close the door on passengers, to drive past people, despite the fact that he is now prohibited by government regulation from having more than a certain number standing.

You can't fit any more on, I sometimes say to him.

He does not listen, and as the doors shut, everyone seems to have miraculously found a space.

I do not know what Simon thinks of his job. I can only guess. He simply takes the money and drives, never talking to passengers, never swearing angrily at other drivers, just doing what he is paid to do.

He has been driving since he was eighteen. Two years ago, he accrued three months' long service leave and took it. I was surprised, even hopeful that perhaps he was planning some change to his life, but he just spent it at home, lying in the darkness of his room watching television.

It's all right, he says on the few occasions when I ask him whether he likes what he does.

Sometimes I am tempted to challenge him, to ask him whether there is anything else he would like to do, but I stop myself in time, not wanting to open things up, not wanting to see him look away, uncomfortable with my question, uncomfortable with me.

Simon took up bus driving two years after he gave up on school.

Vi had tried to talk him into going to a counsellor. It was not so much that he had refused; he had just never turned up for any of the appointments she made. Or if she drove him there, he would go in and not say a word. He would just sit there, completely impenetrable.

At first, the school was also anxious about him.

They, too, tried talking to him, but it was no use, and eventually they gave up.

There's not much point in keeping him here when it's so painfully obvious he has no interest, they told Vi.

He had not handed in a single piece of homework for the entire term. His highest grade in a test had been an E. He no longer talked to any of his friends. He had given up all sport. They didn't know what to do.

Perhaps a year off, the headmaster suggested, although his tone made it clear that it was more than a mere suggestion. *He has obviously been very disturbed by what happened,* and he looked away, not wanting to mention the accident, not wanting to mention Evie's name. *School may only be adding to the stress.*

Vi did not fight.

She, too, didn't really know what to do. Lost in her own grief, she just took the first concrete suggestion that was handed to her.

When Bernard heard, he offered to take Simon out for a man-to-man chat.

He picked him up with Sarah, his girlfriend of the time, and took him sailing. No doubt they would have spent the day on the harbour, drinking champagne and eating prawns, with Bernard tossing Simon the odd cheery comment about what a truly magnificent afternoon it was, losing interest in the response before he had even finished speaking. Simon came home drenched and as silent as ever.

When Vi asked why he was so wet, Bernard laughed. *He's a silly idiot,* and he laughed again, but he looked perplexed as he explained that Sarah's dalmatian had jumped off the boat for a swim and Simon had been convinced she was going to drown. Fully clothed, he had followed her in, trying to save her before they could stop him.

Then Bernard slapped Simon on the back and told him to cheer up. *I don't know why you're looking so glum,* he laughed. *An entire year off – sounds like bliss to me,* and with that he was gone.

So Simon left school.

And he didn't go back.

For the next two years, he stayed at home. Reading, smoking, watching television and eating.

Vi would ask him what he was going to do with his life and Simon would ignore her.

At first her questions weren't so frequent. She was more absorbed in work than ever; having buried herself in causes since the accident, fighting every fight she could, we barely saw her. But after eighteen months, she began to notice that he hadn't moved and seemed to have little intention of doing so.

Rushing out the door to get to a meeting, she would tell him that he shouldn't just waste his life away. Looking up as he tiptoed through her study, trying not to be noticed, she would ask him if he'd thought about going back to school. *Or even a job?* Cleaning out a pile of dirty dishes from his room, she would tell him they needed to talk. *About what was up.*

He would glance across at her. Caught suggesting something that they both knew she was unlikely to do, she would quickly look away.

When I get back, she would say.

Soon, she would add, and she would sigh, anxiously, as she rolled herself another cigarette and tried to work out what to do next.

It was Dawn, one of Vi's old friends from the Equal Work Equal Pay Task Force, who eventually got Simon out of the house. An ex-counsellor for troubled adolescents, she took Simon in hand. And to everyone's surprise, Simon appeared to listen to her.

Vi had been leaving piles of job advertisements inside the

door to Simon's bedroom, research positions, political work, youth work; they all remained where she left them, until eventually she would scoop them up and throw them in the bin.

Dawn told Simon the Department of Transport was recruiting and training drivers, and he agreed to go for an interview.

I am sure that Vi was secretly distressed at the thought of Simon, her son, becoming a bus driver. When he came home and said he had been accepted, she asked him if he was sure this was what he wanted. *Really?*

She tried to console herself with the thought that it was bound to be a temporary measure, until he got through this difficult phase.

But it wasn't.

Twelve years later and Simon still drives buses. Five days a week.

We had arranged to meet at the depot when he finished his shift.

It was still raining and outside the airconditioned office the evening was steamy and unpleasant. Feeling ill from the champagne I had drunk over lunch, I half wished Simon wouldn't turn up and I could go home, but he was there, waiting for me, a copy of the afternoon paper in one hand (a paper that Vi hated) and a cigarette in the other. He was standing under an awning, but apart from that one small concession, he made little attempt to keep dry. I watched as the rain sluiced down, soaking into the newsprint, dripping onto his hair, his arms, and into his shoes. He did not seem to notice.

You haven't changed your mind? he asked me anxiously, and I knew he was referring to the funeral.

I told him I hadn't.

Then why did you want to see me?

I asked him if we could sit down and he led me into a small cafe opposite.

As he pulled out a chair, I saw the heavy perspiration stains under the arms of his shirt and around his neck.

He lit another cigarette.

How do you survive, I asked him, *for all those hours on the bus when you can't smoke?*

He just shrugged his shoulders and looked towards the door, the bell ringing as it opened and closed behind a young woman. She had a baby in a pram, and was heavily pregnant with another. He shifted his chair awkwardly as she tried to push the pram past us. There was no room.

Are you going to eat anything? I asked him, and as I reached across the table for the menu, the baby started crying, the noise high-pitched and insistent.

Simon put his cigarette in the ashtray and leant over. I watched as he pushed the pram back and forth, gently, soothingly. The woman also watched. Waiting up at the counter, she had turned at the first cry and I had seen her about to come back but then stop as Simon reached across. The rocking was working, the baby seemed to be quietening, and as she sat down, she thanked him.

He looked down, embarrassed, apologetic for having acted.

No, thank you, she said again.

And the blush spread further across his face as he scratched at a stain in the formica, head bent, eyes on the table, making me want to reach out and still his hand; making me want to tell him it was okay, he had done the right thing.

He lit another cigarette and I told him I had seen Bernard for lunch. I told him we had talked about the funeral.

He didn't speak.

Why do you want to go? Because I had lowered my voice I was leaning forward, across the table, and as I moved towards him, he pulled back. *I am worried about you.*

The waitress came and I ordered a coffee. Simon ordered a Coke and a chicken sandwich.

I'm thinking of quitting.

I looked at him, surprised. *Why?*

He was staring out the window. *Do you ever think about that time?* he asked me, not wanting to meet my gaze.

I told him I did.

He scratched at the table again, lifting a piece of food with his fingernail and rolling it into a ball.

You know, it wasn't your fault, I said. *The police had to take him away.*

He still wouldn't look at me.

Do you ever think about him much? Mitchell? and he said his name hesitantly, wanting to say it out loud, but unsure, still scared of the effect it would have.

I told him I did. *Quite a bit. Lately.*

My coffee was cold. Weak and milky. I pushed it away.

You can't feel bad about it all, I said, wanting to reassure him. *It was just one of those things,* and I was staring at the ceiling, remembering, imagining, seeing it again: the road, the night, Mitchell.

It was the police who decided what happened, I told him. *Not us. You can't feel guilty.*

I hadn't been there, but I could see it as though I had.

There was a ring of Coke on the table, circling the base of his glass. Black and sticky. Ants. This is what happens when it rains. Thousands of them.

We don't have to go, I said and I wanted him to listen to me. I wanted him to hear me. *You know that, don't you? In fact, it would be better if we didn't. They won't want to see us. There's no reason for us to be there,* and I was leaning forward again, trying to make him look at me.

He did.

You're still coming?

I sat back. There was no point.

Yes, I promised.

And he looked relieved. *I just don't want to be alone,* and he scratched the back of his hand nervously. *It's just,* and he shook his head as he looked away, not wanting to go on.

It's just what? I asked.

He took the last bite of his sandwich and moved his chair back.

Nothing, and he heaved himself up. *I've got to go.*

And knowing that any attempt to make him talk was useless, I told him I'd walk with him.

twenty

When I remember Simon at Candelo, I see him sitting on the verandah with Evie. It is early morning and they are side by side, hip to hip, on the top step. In the sunlight, Simon's hair is blond and his skin is the colour of gold. They each have a bowl of cereal balanced on their lap, soggy with milk, and a glass of juice on the step below them. When Simon takes a spoonful, Evie takes a spoonful, when Simon reaches for his glass, Evie reaches for her glass, when Simon shades his eyes from the sun, Evie shades hers as well, copying each of his movements faithfully.

She reads him jokes from her book, halting over each difficult word.

Why did the tomato blush?

Simon looks suitably perplexed.

Because he saw the salad dressing, and Evie slaps her thigh and laughs uproariously although I am sure she would have had no idea what it meant.

After the fifth joke, I would have told her to shut up.

But Simon doesn't.

He listens until she has had enough.

I see him as he finally gets up and stretches, tall and slim in the clear morning light. Stretching each limb with a grace and lack of self-consciousness that I now find hard to imagine.

Evie does the same.

Simon takes three steps down towards the garden and Evie follows. But when he steps out into the long thick grass, she stops.

It is the snake.

She does not want to go beyond the safety of those stairs. She does not want to move.

Wait, she calls after him and he does.

He turns back towards her. He holds his arms out but she does not follow, although I can see that she wants to, more than anything.

It takes him a few moments before he realises what she is frightened of, and he comes back through the grass, shouting loudly, stomping a flattened path, dark and sparkling with dew.

This is what you do, he tells her and he picks her up so that she is perched high on his shoulders. *You make a lot of noise and you make a path.*

She screams wildly in unison with his shouts, waving her arms in the air as they make their way from one end of the garden to the other.

But when he puts her back down, safe on the stairs, it is clear that she is still worried.

What about tomorrow? she asks. *And the next day?*

He sits next to her. And I hear him as he promises they will do it again. Each morning. They will do it together.

Promise? she asks.

Promise, he says.

I didn't really expect Vi to agree. I didn't expect Simon to come out of the house, the keys glinting in the sun, as he held them up high for us to see.

But he did.

I was sitting on the verandah wall, side by side with Mitchell, learning the art of the perfect smoke ring, practising while we waited for Simon. With his mouth like a fish, Mitchell let each ring form, floating off, invisible in the glare of the day, before passing the cigarette over to me. And with my head arched back, and all my concentration focused on showing him that when it came to smoke rings, I was no fool, I did not hear Simon until he was there, right behind me, the keys held high in one hand.

Got 'em, he told us, and then, seeing me, he looked confused.

I put the cigarette out, hastily stubbing it against the bricks, the tip ground down to grey ash.

You don't smoke, he said.

She's learning, and with his head thrown back and one leg stretched out in front of him, Mitchell imitated me, mercilessly.

I punched him, hard, on the arm.

And he grinned at me.

So, are we going? Simon asked, ignoring us both.

You bet, and Mitchell leapt down onto the grass below, seizing the keys from Simon's hand.

I did not think that Simon would leave me behind. It was not what I would have expected from him, but when I came out with my swimmers in one hand and saw them both laughing, secret jokes on the verandah, I knew they didn't want me with them.

We won't be long, Simon promised and I could see he felt guilty. I could see he was torn, but Mitchell was already starting the engine, and with one foot in, one foot out, Simon was telling me that next time I could go with them; that they wanted to surf, I would be bored, they'd be back in an hour or so, the car door finally slamming shut on his words.

I watched as Mitchell backed away from the house and then, hitting the dirt road, stalled. He turned the ignition again, revving the engine. *Warming it up,* he shouted back to me, his words carrying to where I stood. I could not see him but I could imagine his wink, as, with one last rev, he eventually drove off, disappearing down the dip in the road.

And sitting on that verandah, I felt bored and alone.

Go for a walk, Vi said when I told her I had nothing to do. *Take Evie with you.* My mother always found boredom incomprehensible. It is a luxury that she used to say she longed for, although I doubt whether she ever meant it.

I was sitting on the edge of her bed watching her type. Her ashtray was full and the floor was already covered with papers and books.

Can't you come? I asked her.

She butted out another cigarette and finished her sentence, her thin fingers rapid on the keys. Carriage return. Pause.

And she looked up at me, unsure as to what I had said.

I repeated my question.

She was staring into the distance, thinking of her next

paragraph, working it out, her brow furrowed in concentration.

Half an hour, she told me and she began typing again, furiously, not looking up as I sighed, heavily. Not looking up as I closed the door to her room with what I hoped was a pointed slam.

I knew what half an hour meant. Two hours. Maybe three.

Evie was asleep. Curled up at the bottom of a cupboard, surrounded by old games – Chinese checkers, ludo, cards, faded cardboard that had curled and browned at the edges scattered around her. I did not wake her. I hadn't really wanted her company anyway.

And walking out along the dirt road, I wondered how much of this holiday I would have to spend alone.

It was hot. Hot and still, and beneath my feet the gravel crunched with each step, stones flicking up behind me and hitting the backs of my legs. If I paused for even a moment, the flies were thick. Black and ugly, swarming across my arms and in my eyes.

When I left the road, I didn't really know where I was heading. I just walked towards the line of willows in the distance, a ribbon of dusty green against the faded hills that swelled behind them. I cut through a paddock, lifting up the barbed-wire fence with one hand while I swung my legs through the gap. The ground was uneven and dry, pocked with crusty cow pats. From a distance these paddocks looked like velvet, but close the grass was like straw, sharp against my ankles.

I hadn't expected to end up at the creek. I had just walked with my head down, carefully watching each step, so that I heard it before I saw it. The water trickling over rocks and the gentle brush of the sagging willow branches across the surface of the stream that wound its way through the sandy banks on either side.

The water was shallow. From where I stood I could see the bottom, smooth pebbles dappled with light.

I looked around quickly before taking my shorts and T-shirt off and stepping slowly out to the middle, the deepest point reaching my waist.

Lying back with my head against one of the rocks, I let the water wash over me. Above, the sky was brilliant blue, spliced into diamonds by the drooping branches of the trees. And as I stared up, high up, I found that I was thinking of Mitchell. With the warmth of the sun on the tops of my legs and the cool water rushing underneath me, I could see him, sitting next to me on the verandah wall, his thigh resting against mine. Dark-brown eyes staring out from the shaggy fringe of blond hair. Square-tipped fingers and the flick of his cigarette out across the verandah. Smooth tanned skin, the straight flat line of his stomach.

And slowly I let myself sink down, deep down, my hair cool and wet down my back.

Coming up for air.

Before sinking down again.

Down to where it was cool and quiet.

And I imagined.

All of it.

With the slow swoop of the branches overhead.

Backwards and forwards.

Skimming the surface of the creek.

twenty-one

There was a time, before Evie was born, when I was obsessed with quantifying Vi's love for us.

Who do you love best? I would ask her, over and over again.

When she would tell me that she loved us equally, I would become all the more insistent.

But you must love one of us more, I would say, determined to push her towards the answer that I feared, determined to make her say that it was Simon, Simon who was loved best, Simon who was the favourite.

Sitting under her desk, I used to take out the photo albums and look back over a past that had little meaning for me, despite the fact that it was my past. Faded black and white prints of Vi and Bernard on their wedding day, Vi awkward in a white hat with feathers, gloves and a tiny handbag. Bernard with his arm around her, smiling with the full force of his charm into the camera. Their first house together, picnics on the headland, Vi lying back on a rug, Bernard feeding her strawberries. I would turn the pages rapidly, the tissue thin and dry between my fingers, until I came to the ones I wanted.

The baby photos.

Pages and pages of Simon.

Two of me.

See, I would tell her, crawling out from where I had been sitting, tugging at her hand so that she would be forced to stop typing.

She would look down momentarily, uncertain as to what it was that I was showing her, and then turn back to what she was doing. But it wouldn't stop me. I would count them out for her: twenty-eight pictures of Simon, five of me.

When she finally realised that I wasn't going to let it go, she would sit me down and tell me about first and second children, her voice patient and well modulated. A voice she might have learnt from a family therapy book. *It's not that we loved you less,* she would explain. *But when you were born, Simon was only two and we just didn't have the time.*

If I dared to ask her now, I wonder whether she would be more honest with me. I wonder whether she would talk about the gentleness in Simon. I wonder whether she would talk about the desire to protect that she always had with him. I do not know. Because to talk about these things would be to hold up their life now. In the same house, but never in the same room, Simon awkward in doorways, wanting to help but unable to, Vi darting nervously around him, a rapid fire of words with no substance as she picks up after him and then is gone without ever having met his eyes once. Short notes left on the sideboard, Simon appearing for meals and then taking them up to his room, Simon sitting at the table, eyes fixed on the paper in front of him.

When I talk of Vi, people tell me I am lucky. *You speak the same language,* they say.

And we do. We know each other.

Half-finished sentences collide with no need for completion, giant leaps take us to the same place at the same time, irritation flares and then dissipates, one of us lies and the other one knows: this is the bond that we share.

But.

It has never meant that we reveal everything to each other.

I stand in Vi's garden and I pick herbs for our dinner. Sweet basil, sage and peppery rocket, the last leaves left from the summer. All planted and cared for by Mari.

I was lucky with my children, I once overheard Vi say. *They didn't fight with each other.*

And we didn't. Not really. Any attempt I made to fight with Simon would always be stymied by his good nature.

They liked being with each other.

And I did. I would follow him, wanting to be a part of whatever it was he was doing, wanting to be there, once again reliant on his good nature, trusting it enough to know that he would not turn me away.

Which was how he was. Until Candelo. Until Mitchell.

As I search for the last of the lettuce, I find myself pulling out the weeds that have begun to grow since Mari has spent more and more of her time looking after Vi. I toss them into a heap, knowing that I am doing this because I do not want to go back inside. I do not want to have another meal with

126

Simon sitting there, silent at one end of the table, eating rapidly, and leaving immediately.

And as I tug and pull at clumps of sticky green nettles, careful to avoid what I recognise to be plants, I think about what I would be like as a mother. I think about the choices Vi made, and I am overwhelmed by the relentless slide of generations, each replacing the next.

Her gone and me in her shoes.

And the decision I have had to make weighs heavily on me.

twenty-two

They did not get home until just before dark.

I doubt whether Vi would have noticed if I hadn't kept asking her where they were. But as the heat of the afternoon burnt into a soft dusk, as I asked her again and again, she began to look at the clock. She was irritated. And it was building.

I was giving Evie a bath when I heard the front door slam, followed by Simon calling out, letting us know they were back.

Evie struggled and squirmed out of my hold. She was out of the bath and running, dripping wet, up the hall towards them before I could stop her.

Hey there, sexy legs. The broadness of Mitchell's voice rang through the house as Evie threw herself on them, both of them.

I'm in the raw, she shouted and I heard the three of them laughing as Evie danced down towards the kitchen with Mitchell behind her, aping each of her moves, kicking his legs out, waving his hands in the air.

I was angry with them. Still. And standing by the bathroom

door, I tried to look unamused but I, too, could not help but laugh, as I watched Mitchell wag his head from side to side, his hair stiff with salt and sand, his face sunburnt, his mouth open in a smile that threatened to split his face in two.

It was Vi who didn't find it funny.

She was in the kitchen, sitting at the table under the harsh fluoro light, as they came to a stop, bags of groceries at their feet, there in front of her.

I waited for what would follow, part of me wanting trouble. I watched Evie tug slyly, once, twice, at Mitchell's hand, wanting the game to continue, before she, too, realised the fun was over.

Vi brushed her hair back from her forehead, took her glasses off, and folded her arms.

She was silent for a moment.

And then she told them.

She had never said they could have the car all afternoon. In fact, she might have wanted to use it.

She was very angry.

She was disappointed.

I listened and I watched their faces. We all knew she hadn't wanted to go anywhere, but this was what Vi was like. She had decided she was angry and the accuracy of the reason was of little importance.

She uncorked the red wine and poured herself a glass without offering one to any of us.

At least you remembered to do the shopping, and she pulled the food furiously out of the bags that lay at her feet.

It was Simon who went to help her.

Mitchell stayed where he was, leaning against the doorframe, tapping his foot and scratching nervously at his forearm.

Evie winked at him and he winked back. Evie stuck her tongue out at him and he stuck his out at her. They were both trying not to laugh. Suppressing it.

But it was his eyes that gave him away.

Glassy. Red.

Out of it.

I quickly glanced at Simon. He was grinning, from ear to ear.

And I wondered how long it would take before Vi noticed. Sometimes she was oblivious to what was going on, but at other times, she didn't miss a thing. Sometimes she couldn't have cared, at others, the slightest infraction was cause for raging fury.

It was Evie who gave the game away. Her face close to Simon's as he unpacked the bags, she recoiled in disgust. *You stink.* She turned to me. *Smell him, Ursula.*

I told her to shoosh, but it was too late.

Vi looked at both of them. Neither of them were quick enough to duck their heads from her gaze.

For Christ's sake, and she slammed a tin of tomatoes onto the table. *I really would have expected more sensible behaviour.*

But you let us smoke, Simon said, feebly.

She snapped back at him: *Not when you're driving,* and she turned to Mitchell. *If this isn't going to work, then we'd better face up to it now and get you on the next train.* He lowered his head.

If I treat you like an adult, I expect you to behave like one. I can't believe you would be so bloody stupid.

He muttered an apology.

Perhaps we'd better just call it quits, and she lit a cigarette, grinding the dead match into the ashtray as she spoke.

I looked at Simon. I couldn't bring myself to look at Mitchell.

You're not being fair. You're blaming it all on him, and Simon fidgeted nervously with the sleeve of his shirt.

She just stared at him.

It was my idea. I was the one who suggested it.

I waited.

It wasn't his fault.

She looked across at Mitchell.

He didn't even want any.

Vi snorted in disbelief. *And you held him down and forced him?*

I watched as Mitchell shifted awkwardly from one foot to the other. There was a fine film of sand coating his heels, a trail that led up to his Achilles tendon and petered out at the base of his calves.

Finally he spoke. He looked across at her and told her he was sorry. He just hadn't thought. He didn't know what to say.

From above, the buzz of the fluorescent light seemed unbearably loud.

I noticed that Evie still didn't have any clothes on and I took her hand. *Pyjamas,* I said, and she tried to wriggle out of my grasp.

We'll make dinner, Simon offered.

Vi took her cardigan from the back of the chair and tied it round her shoulders.

She was going to have a walk. To the road and back. To

cool down. And she stubbed out her cigarette and downed the last of her wine, leaving the room without looking back.

Don't worry, Simon said. *She'll get over it.*

And he and Mitchell looked at each other before collapsing into a fit of giggles.

Jesus, and Mitchell bent over double, holding the arm of the chair, *I thought we were done for.*

I stared at both of them in disbelief.

You know, and Mitchell picked up the shopping from the floor, *your mum's pretty cool. For an old bird.*

And as he collapsed once more into laughter, I couldn't help but smile, and with the start of my smile, I, too, found I was laughing, reluctantly at first, and then louder.

Until we were all laughing. Simon, Evie, Mitchell and I.

Backs pressed against the wall, holding our sides, unable to look at each other.

And laughing.

'In loving memory of Mitchell Jenkins.'

I read obituaries in the paper and I wonder what they wrote about Mitchell. I wonder who spoke for him. If there was only one. Or columns of messages.

In loving memory.

I don't know what my memory is. One minute I tell Lizzie that I loved him and I remember the intensity of my crush, burning, and then I want to retract my words. It wasn't love. It seems such a stupid word to have used.

Because my memory is so confused, I do not know how I would describe it. I am, at times, overwhelmed with shame.

I can feel it drain me, empty me, until I am paper dry, flat and without weight.

In loving memory.

And my throat closes tight as I remember.

Mitchell Jenkins.

He woke me in the middle of the night.

Tapping in the stillness on the glass door that separated our rooms.

Ursula, his voice a hiss in the quiet.

Outside, the sky was clear. Sprayed with stars. Thousands of them smattered across the darkness. And it was still warm. A soft breeze in the cypress trees, giant dark towers marking the small space that had once been garden, home, to someone, sometime ago.

Ursula.

At first I thought it was a dream, a voice from the depths of my sleep, calling me, and I did not move, I just let it whisper. Over and over.

The tapping on the glass.

Like rain.

But there was no rain.

And as I opened my eyes, I saw him there, on the other side, hissing my name in the still of the night.

Half asleep, I tiptoed down the hall and out the front door, his shadowy figure there in front of me, leading me. *This way.* Trying not to walk into things, not sure where I was, not sure if he was sleepwalking or I was, just following, right behind him, opening the front door to the night sky, leading me through, and out to the verandah, down the steps, our feet in the dampness of the grass. *Here,* he said, and we sat, side by side, there on the bottom stair, with nothing but us and the night, black and still, before us.

I wanted to see the stars, he whispered, and I did not know what to say.

With my knees tucked to my chest, I held myself, tightly, rocking myself, as though it was cold, but it wasn't cold. Each faint breath of air was warm and silky.

And I watched as he rolled a joint, the quick movement of his fingers, back and forth, until it was smooth and white, complete in his hands. And as he lit it, the tip glowed, fierce in the dark, fiery against the black emptiness in front of us.

I've never been to a place like this before, he whispered, letting out a thin stream of smoke with each word, and he waved his arm, the end of the joint like a pointer in the dark.

I could feel his thigh next to mine. The smooth hairs on his legs. And I did not move.

Imagine, all this, and he tilted his head back, breathing in, closing his eyes for one instant, *owning all this, and not even living here.*

And as he passed the joint to me, the tips of his fingers brushed mine. *You know, at my mum's flat, there's no garden, not even a balcony,* his words soft, whispered to himself, not looking at me, just staring out at the night, the shapes of the trees more visible, our eyes slowly opening to it all.

I looked at him.

He watched as I drew back.

Hold it in, he told me.

I did.

When I get back, his words a faint whisper, right there, next to me, *it's gonna be different. I'm going to get a job, my own place, make some money,* and he sighed, *then maybe, some day, I'll come and live in a place like this.*

He looked at me as I passed the joint back to him, and I watched as he pinched it between thumb and forefinger, drawing back with a sharp intake of breath.

What are you going to do, oh, Ur-su-la? and he grinned as he pronounced each syllable of my name separately, sing-song, the smoke coming out from the base of his throat in one thick stream.

Well, Mitch-ell, and I giggled, *I think I'm going to be a famous actor, or a writer or a singer.*

He laughed. *Piece of piss.*

That's what I reckon, I told him.

What about your brother? he asked.

I stared up, high up, at the night sky and tried to see the patterns that I knew were there. *An artist,* I said. *He's going to be an artist,* and I did not know if I should say any more. I did not know if Simon would want me to tell.

And Evie?

I shrugged my shoulders and looked out across the garden, the gate now visible, and beyond that the road, and somewhere that line of willows, and beneath that, the creek. *I don't know,* I told him. *She could be anything.*

Anything at all, he said.

And in the silence, I watched him lean forward, looking straight ahead. *You know what my sister does?* he asked.

I didn't.

Manages a shop. Menswear. She got away from home young. Left us as soon as she could.

And he moved towards me, just for a moment, hesitating, everything still as I waited and he waited, both of us, unsure, so brief, that I found myself wondering if it had ever happened. *Good luck to you,* his voice soft, and the grass damp between my toes, just the light from the stars and the tip of that joint, with the house behind us, solid and dark, and the pair of us, sitting side by side, hip to hip, on that step.

I think it's gone out, I whispered, holding it between my fingers.

And as he leant forward to light it again, I watched as the match burnt and then flickered out.

Because his mouth was on mine.

And I could feel his hand brushing, a slow rush, just the surface, the inside of my leg.

And I didn't want him to stop. The warmth of his mouth, the smokiness of his breath, the cool grass beneath my feet and the brush of his hand, all of it, while overhead the night was still and dark.

I've gotta go, I whispered.

Why?

I couldn't answer.

And as I shifted my leg from his, as I stood up, I felt the cool that comes just before dawn, unlocking my fingers from his and turning to walk back up the stairs, towards the house, unable to tell him that it was too much. All of it.

So I didn't say anything.

I just left him, the door clicking softly as I opened it, closing it behind me, leaving him out there.

Alone on the bottom step.

With the night slowly lifting towards day.

twenty-three

Vi still believes in marriage. Despite the fact that it was clearly a disaster for her.

Sometimes she stops what she is doing and looks up from the box she is sorting. She lifts her glasses onto the top of her head. Her eyes are cloudy now. Where they were sharp and intense, dark stones, they are milky at the edges and the whites have yellowed.

She stares across at me and I know she is about to make one of her pronouncements. I brace myself.

Her voice has always been deep, but it has lost some of its richness and it cracks, breaking in the middle of certain syllables, as she tells me that it would be a pity if I didn't get married.

Really, she says and she reaches for my hand.

I try to explain that I don't see any need for marriage, that it is not an institution that means a great deal to me, nor, I would have thought, to her, but she doesn't listen.

You don't have to take all that dogma so seriously, and she waves her hand through the air, impatiently, dismissively. *Marriage is whatever you want it to be.*

I can't help but remind her that it was hardly one of her life successes.

That was your father, she tells me with some irritation.

I ask her what is wrong with living with someone.

Nothing, she says. *Nothing at all. It's just not the same.* And then she looks at me again, and tells me that she wasn't intending to be disparaging about my relationship with Marco.

I know, I say, irritated with her now.

The way I felt about Marco is a totally separate issue. I know it was serious for you and I am not dismissing that.

I bend down to a box and start pulling out the next bundle of files, dusty and creased at the edges, not wanting to look at her and not wanting to continue this conversation.

I know she never really liked Marco. She never used to tell me this, but when he finally left, she said that she had always thought he was *wrong for me.*

I was surprised. With his impeccable working-class credentials, I would have thought he was perfect.

You never had that spark, she said. *You were never right together,* and then she turned back to whatever it was that she had been doing at the time.

She was right.

Not that I had ever talked to her about our relationship. I doubt whether I ever even told her I had started seeing him. His name just replaced the person before, just as his had replaced someone else's name before him.

But with Marco, I did try. I wanted something solid. I did

like him and, on the whole, we got on well. He was good to me. The problem lay not just in our fights, nor in our differences, which were probably no worse than most people's. There was, as Vi so delicately put it, a lack of spark.

Why don't you ever want to have sex? Marco would complain as I would push him away, again and again.

How do you tell someone that you are not attracted to them?

There was something in the heaviness of his body, in the thick solidity of him, that I felt would smother me, suffocate me, and I would pull away.

But how was I meant to say that?

So I would lie, over and over again, until even the times when I did give in, when I would sink into his arms, even when I wanted to, would seem a lie.

When I told Marco it was over, that there was someone else, he asked me who it was.

I refused to say.

Is it serious? he asked.

I said I didn't know, it might just be a sex thing; it was too early to tell.

He looked at me dumbfounded. *But you're not interested in sex,* and there was complete disbelief in his voice.

And then he hated me for what I had done to him.

Because he, too, had lied to himself. He had refused to see how things were.

I would kiss Anton in secret. I would meet him where no one would see us. I would wait until I heard Louise's footsteps on the path. I would plot and I would plan.

You can't tell, Anton had said, horrified, when I had told him it was finished with Marco. *About us.*

Sitting out on the edge of the cliff, watching the afternoon light hit the north point, his face, which in its reflection had been so alive, so mobile, froze with fear. Holding his hand but knowing he was no longer there. Feeling his fingers in mine and then feeling them uncurl, one by one, feeling the shift in his body, away from me.

And as I lay in my bed and remembered this, as I thought about the decision I was making, I noticed that the rain had stopped.

It was the quiet that had woken me, the still that had come after what seemed to be days of a relentless downpour. Nothing. Just the sound of the sea.

I got up and I opened my front door. I could smell the freshness of the night. It was clear now, clear enough to see the stars.

At the end of the building I could see the light on in Mouse's room. He never turns it off. It burns all day and all night. I have never asked him why. And as I stood on my doorstep, one foot in, one foot out, the door to Mouse's flat opened, slowly.

We looked at each other.

Still up? he asked.

Can't sleep, I told him.

He was smoking a joint. He held it out towards me. Beneath my feet, the path was still damp. I walked towards him, and I took it from his fingers without a word.

I looked up at the night sky and I remembered. Sitting out

on the steps with Mitchell. All those years ago. Waving his hands in the air, the tip like a pointer in the darkness.

I turned to Mouse and then looked behind me at the emptiness of his flat. *Burgled?* I asked him.

He took the joint from my hand.

Yeah, and he drew back, sucking it in, holding it in.

This is what happens to Mouse. All the time. It is usually one of the many who knock on his door late at night, shouting out his name: *Mouse, Mouse, let me in.*

Find the guy?

He shook his head.

And we smoked in silence, not speaking as we watched the night sky slowly fade; tentative sunlight after days of rain.

twenty-four

Sometimes in the morning it is difficult to think about what you have done the night before. It is difficult to reconcile those actions with who you are during the day.

I left Mitchell sitting on the steps as the darkness slowly faded.

I lay curled up in my bed, listening to Evie asleep next to me. I was tired but not tired. I was wrapped in the thought of him, wrapped in the feel of him, wanting to sleep, but wanting to stay awake, as it all floated, exciting and terrifying, backwards and forwards through my mind.

And that was how I stayed, as I listened to the birds singing in the trees outside the window, sharp and piercing, cutting through the first morning light, the first pink in the sky, the clarity of the blue, until at last I fell asleep, closing my eyes to the sounds of the others getting up.

When I woke it was past midday. When I woke the sun was high, burning hot in the sky. I looked at the empty room.

I heard the still of the house. And I did not want to think about what had happened the night before.

The note on the kitchen table told me they had all gone to the beach. They would be back in the afternoon.

I was surprised Vi had gone, and I checked her room. The neatly made bed, the piles of papers, the books covering the floor, the stale smell of the ashtray, the row of high-heeled shoes.

I turned on her transistor and twisted the dial away from the national radio station to the local one, the tinny sound of pop music blaring out as I sat on her bed and lit one of her cigarettes.

The taste was foul. My throat was dry and thick, but I did not put it out; I persisted. Watching myself smoke in the speckled, scratched mirror that hung on the front of the wardrobe. My reflection swam in the glass. Yellow and hazy. And I stood up and stepped back. To see all of me. Narrowing my eyes. Imagining myself in another body confronted with me, there, in front of me.

The sunlight was slanting in through the doors that opened onto the courtyard, making it difficult to see who I really was, to see any more than just an outline. Short, skinny; curly black hair. I leant closer to the mirror, blowing out the smoke in a thick choking haze that hit the glass and dispersed in a grey fog. Peering closer. Dark eyes like Vi's, big mouth, long slightly hooked nose.

You have a face that you will grow into, Vi once said to me. *You'll see.*

I drew back on the cigarette and held it in, watching myself, turning to one side and then the other, smiling as I flicked the ash into the ashtray.

I had once asked Simon if he thought I was good-looking.

What do you mean? he had said.

It was the day I had first kissed a boy. After school, behind the library. A dare. We had to do it for five minutes, in front of an audience. When we had finished, he had followed me home, finally summoning the courage to ask me if I wanted to go to the pictures with him.

I didn't.

It was his best friend I liked. And he only had eyes for Alana Smythe, tall, blonde and tanned.

You're just you, Simon had said.

But am I good-looking? I had persisted. *If you weren't my brother, would you like me?*

But I am your brother, he had said, finding it impossible to comprehend my question.

I looked at my legs in the mirror, pulling my shorts up to reveal the tops of my thighs.

I lifted my T-shirt and looked at my breasts. Small, barely there.

Vi had laughed when I had asked her if I could buy a bra.

What on earth for?

All the other girls had them.

And when I had shaved my legs for the first time, she had given me a long lecture on male fantasies, male desires, male notions of how a woman should look and act.

Then why do you wear high shoes? And those dresses?

She had told me she was old enough to make her own

decisions. She wore what she wanted to wear; she had never dressed for a man and she never would.

But what if I like smooth legs? I had persisted.

She had told me I was being ridiculous. There was no hair there in the first place. She didn't want to argue any more.

Similarly, when I first got my period, I asked her to buy me some pads. She came back from the shop with a box of tampons.

I can't use those, I had said.

I had heard the girls at school. You could lose your virginity if you used a tampon, their mothers would never let them, and as for the idea of putting your finger inside yourself – they would wrinkle their noses in disgust.

Vi told me to stop being so silly, and she laid the instructions out across the kitchen table, leaving me to work them out.

I put my cigarette out and lit another one.

Practice.

The taste was not getting any better. But my technique definitely was.

And I sat out in the heat of the courtyard, where the weeds pushed up through the stone flagging, where the sun could tan my legs, where I could still see myself in the reflection of the glass doors.

But out there in the brightness of that day, in the sharpness of that sunlight, staring up at the sky, I would find the night before slowly creeping back in. And I would catch my breath, just for a moment, with the whisper of a blade of grass, a leaf brushing the side of my legs, I would feel it all come back and I would close my eyes and stop breathing. Because all that was day, all that was solid seemed to slide away from me, drain like blood, until I was there again under the night sky with his mouth on mine.

Their room was on the other side of the courtyard. Their door squeaked as I opened it. Rotten wood straining on rusted hinges. Their beds were unmade, their clothes were scattered across the floor.

The glass door that separated them from Evie and me was closed.

I had watched them through it, their light on, ours off. Their bodies illuminated. Ours in darkness. Stripped down to their underpants. Simon, tall and slim, still like a boy. Long-limbed and slender. Mitchell, also thin, but with a breadth in his chest and strength in his arms.

I looked at his things and I looked at Simon's, already blending into each other – socks, jeans, T-shirts, tangled together. I picked through them, wanting to find some clue as to who he was.

The indent of the mattress from where he had slept.

The twist of the sheets at the foot of the bed.

Cigarette butts in a saucer.

A silver marijuana leaf on a piece of leather thonging.

A torch that was sticky-taped together.

All this.

And nothing.

I followed Evie's path, the one that Simon had made for her that morning, across the front garden and out onto the dirt road, turning towards what remained of the orchard at the side of the house.

The trees were gnarled and twisted, stunted by years of neglect, with small clusters of tart apples and woody pears. I climbed the nearest, as high as I could go, perching myself up there so I could see it all. The red roof of the house, the gentle roll of the paddocks, the bare branches of the gums, streaky-barked, the tumble of boulders down the side of a hill, the line of willows that marked what I knew to be the river, and the twist of the yellow dirt road, winding its way back to Candelo, to the highway, to the coast, to where the waves crashed against the shore.

I wanted to be able to see when they came back.

But I did not want them to see me.

I did not want him to see me.

Not straightaway.

And with my back against the smooth branch, I stayed there, listening to the rush of the leaves overhead, letting myself drift in and out of the day that I was in and the night that had just passed.

twenty-five

When I made my decision, it was not as though there was a decision to make. It was suddenly clear. The indecision I had been lost in no longer made sense. It no longer seemed possible that I could not know.

I sat on the damp front step of Mouse's flat, sharing a joint and remembering Mitchell, and as I looked out across the garden, as I watched each tree, each bush slowly taking shape in the beginnings of the day, I knew that I could not do it. Not on my own.

Letting myself into my flat, I saw it all in the half-light from the window. Two small rooms, with my clothes on the floor, my books stacked underneath the windows, the dishes in the sink, the chaos that had surrounded me since Marco had left. The chaos that was there before he had turned up in my life. The chaos in which he had attempted, unsuccessfully, to make a small dent, an impression of change.

Outside, the sun was now streaking the ocean crimson, the line of sky skirting the horizon impossibly rich in its blue.

When we first started living together, I would wake Marco to look at the dawn.

I had never watched that transition from night to day with Anton. We had never had a full night together. But I had with Marco, often. He would open his eyes momentarily, grunt in appreciation, and then go back to sleep. I would stay up watching, the great ball clinging to the lip of the sea, held there for just a moment, before it slowly separated, rising towards morning.

As I closed the curtains so that I could sleep, I saw myself, momentarily, reflected in the window.

I did not have the courage.

I was a fool for ever thinking I had.

And when I woke, three hours later, I rang the clinic and made an appointment.

She gave me a day and a time. She told me not to drive and she told me to bring clean underpants and sanitary pads.

I hung up and did not know what to do next.

It was the day before the funeral and I had no work. No audition to prepare for. No friends I had arranged to visit. Nothing.

I heard Mouse slamming the bathroom door and I heard Louise coming down the path and past my door. As I got up and searched for my swimmers on the floor, I heard her going up the wooden stairs, sagging after all the rain; I heard her key in the lock, her footsteps down the hall, in their bedroom, and the thud of her shoes as she took them off, one by one, and climbed into bed to try to sleep.

The path to the beach was still wet. Dripping branches had been tossed, pulled and flattened, making certain places almost impenetrable. Clumps of blood-red lilies with thick purple leaves bent at their stems. Nasturtiums and morning glory in a tangled heap of destruction, and great pools of rain that soaked up through my sandshoes.

Below me I could hear the sea.

I could hear it before I saw it.

The thunder of the waves, white and wild, over the rocks, slapping up against the base of the path, almost licking the edge and then pulling back.

And I stood there, looking out, watching the ocean and, in the distance, Anton, walking towards me. Watching him without realising it was him. Seeing him just as I would see anyone coming back from a swim, hair still wet, towel over his shoulder, T-shirt damp.

He looked at me and I looked at him.

And I did not know whether he, too, remembered the times we would meet on the stairs, when we would swim together, when he would tell me that he had hoped he would find me waiting for him.

Rough, he said, searching for conversation but only finding that one word.

I know, I said, equally devoid of anything to say.

Salt clung to the tips of his eyelashes, white on black. Seaweed still curled around his wrist.

How are you feeling? he asked, and it was the kind of question I would expect from him. General. Floating. Failing to alight on what was at hand.

I told him I was fine, and as I moved to walk past him, he put his hand on my arm.

Can't we talk? he asked. *Not today, Louise is at home, but tomorrow?*

His fingers, still icy from the sea, were wrapped around my wrist, heavy and cold. I moved away. I took one step back and I told him I was busy tomorrow, I had a funeral to go to, I had nothing to say.

And as the waves slapped against the path, he tried to tell me how sorry he was. He tried to say he had never wanted this to happen, but each sentence seemed to drift off, useless words carried away with the breeze, until finally he just said he was sorry again.

And I could see he was.

But it didn't mean much. Coming this late.

He moved to go and I watched him walk away, just for a moment, until he disappeared around the bend in the stairs, and I turned back towards the ocean, towards the pool.

twenty-six

Vi has always believed that you should talk to young people as adults, that you should treat them as equals.

I have seen her with children, young children, answering their questions with an earnestness that makes no sense to them.

Why? they ask, over and over again, and Vi will explain, in detail, usually managing to slip a political message into her answer.

As we got older, she thought it was important to keep up to date with what interested us: music, films, books. She would try to ask questions. She would set aside time to get to know us.

I could not bear it. When she made an effort. To relate.

What's this you're listening to? she would ask, putting her head around my bedroom door.

Music, I would tell her.

And she would respond with equal sarcasm. *Really?*

Although Simon also saw through her attempts, he would

usually try harder. He would tell her who it was. He would even get out the cover and show her, or perhaps play her something else. She would sit and listen, occasionally tapping her foot in time to the beat, nodding her head in appreciation, until after a few moments it was clear that she was bored and wanted to get back to work.

Vi tried with Mitchell. To enter his world. To talk to him on his level.

And it was excruciating.

I could hear her as I let myself into the house, her voice deep and earnest, echoing from the kitchen up the long dusty corridor, and I cringed.

They were back from the beach. United by sunburn, sand and the sea, they barely noticed I was there.

Saved you some, and Simon glanced up for a moment as he pointed at the fish and chips, cold and greasy, spread across the kitchen table.

Evie was kneeling on her chair with her clothes stuffed up her T-shirt, pulling faces at Simon and Mitchell. Vi was leaning against the cupboard, her hair awry from swimming, a hint of colour in her face, as she rolled another cigarette and asked Mitchell about his interests; her face intent and serious as he told her the bands he liked, as he listed them for her.

I knew she didn't know any of them, but she nodded all the same, knowledgeably, occasionally turning to Simon, *You like them too,* seeking confirmation that she knew what Mitchell was talking about.

It was when she asked him if he was interested in a career in music that he grinned, the white of his teeth startling against the tan on his face as he thought about the combination of those two words, 'career' and 'music'.

Don't know, he said, the possibility of it opening up before him. Exciting him. *How?* he asked.

Vi wasn't stumped. *What about some of the community arts access programs in your area? There have been some excellent ones started up by this government.*

Mitchell looked at her blankly. *Sure,* and he winked at Evie who was silently mouthing each of Vi's words, imitating her with her unerring accuracy.

Still by the door, out of Vi's sight, I rolled my eyes at Simon, who looked away quickly. Quelling the laughter.

It might be worth finding out more about them. I've come across a few kids who started young rock bands that way.

When? I asked, louder than I had intended, so that they all turned.

And as Mitchell looked straight at me, I blushed, hating myself for the slow rush of colour that began near my ears, moving across my face, forcing me to look down, away from him, away from all of them. Because I was sure they could see. They must have been able to see.

You, a famous movie star, and me, a rock star, he stared at me. *Why not?*

Exactly, and Vi glared at me.

Later, Simon and I were imitating her, Vi, and her knowledge of music.

Your mum's not so bad, Mitchell said.

I told him she was a dickhead.

Nah, she's pretty cool.

We were putting away the dishes. Mitchell, unable to simply take plates to the cupboard, was spinning each piece of crockery in his hands, twirling cups on one finger, throwing bowls in the air and catching them, drumming spoons on the table edge, so that I found myself holding my breath with each dish I handed him.

What's your mum called? Evie asked him, looking up from where she was colouring in at the table.

I watched as Mitchell put down the saucers he had been piling too high in his hands. One by one. Silent for a moment. Pausing before answering. Looking out the window as he spoke. *My mum's dead.*

And I was surprised.

No she's not, I said, because I was sure he had mentioned his mother the night before. The flat where she lived.

Simon kicked me and I glared at him, wanting to protest, wanting to say that it wasn't true, his mother was alive, but I didn't. I didn't want to mention the conversation I had had with Mitchell, just the two of us, out there on the steps.

And I was confused. I didn't know what was truth and what wasn't.

When? Evie asked, and with her face turned towards him, she waited for an answer.

Simon and I also waited. All of us waiting for him to speak. He didn't.

When? she asked again as he leant forward, and she pulled back, uncertain for one instant as to what he was about to do.

All of us uncertain.

Wanting her to shut up.

But she wouldn't. Not Evie.

When? she giggled, as he seized her in both hands, as he picked her up and put her on his shoulders, her textas clattering to the ground as she screamed in delight.

And when he finally spoke, his words were not an answer to her question.

We're outta here, he told her.

Outta here, she agreed.

The noise in his throat like the throttle of an engine, slowly building to a roar, he ducked low under the back door, and then was off, gone, racing Evie out across the night black of the back garden, while Simon and I watched, both of us staring out through the cracked glass of the window.

See, I said.

See what? Simon didn't look at me, his eyes still fixed on the pair of them, only just visible out there without us. He seemed to have barely even heard me.

I opened my mouth, I was about to speak, about to explain that Mitchell hadn't even told us when she had died, that she wasn't dead, but then I stopped myself.

It doesn't matter, I said, knowing he hadn't heard me, knowing he had already forgotten what I had been talking about.

And I let it go.

Until later, when I brought it up again.

We were playing cards. Pontoon in their bedroom. Simon, Mitchell and I. Evie with her own deck, dealing anything to herself as she imitated our game. *Hit me. Hit me,* until she had a pile in front of her.

Mitchell had brought in the rest of Vi's wine from dinner

and we drank from the bottle, passing it round, each taking long slow swills.

You can't bet all your matches, Simon told me as I pushed the pile forward.

Why not?

Because if you lose, you'll be out of the game.

He was banker, cautious, slow, building a pile. I had already been bankrupt three times, borrowing from him, borrowing from Mitchell, feeling the flush of the wine on my cheeks as I kept on bidding, up and up.

You can't keep borrowing, he protested. *It makes the whole game pointless.*

Why? I asked, belligerent with the alcohol.

Evie was now curled up at the foot of Mitchell's mattress, her thumb in her mouth, the deck of cards scattered around her. She stirred as we argued, shifting in half-sleep, until Simon picked her up and carried her through to the other room, leaving us alone.

For just a moment.

And we sat on the floor under the bare light of the globe. Side by side, facing the space where Simon had been.

Neither of us sure what to say.

Until, too confident from the alcohol, I spoke without thinking. *Why did you lie about your mum?* I asked him, dividing my matches up into piles and then re-dividing, smaller and smaller.

He wouldn't look at me.

I watched him butt out his cigarette, grinding it into the saucer. He was squinting, perplexed and awkward, jiggling his knee up and down, up and down. I could see where the ash had stained his finger, smudged grey across the white of the scar. I could see the smooth line of his calf muscle, the fall of his hair across his cheek, the full width of his mouth.

And I was aware of the strangeness of his silence. Because it was not like Mitchell to be this quiet.

But I didn't stop.

I told him I didn't understand. What he had said about his mother's flat. The night before. It made no sense. I told him he could tell me. I told him I wanted to know. I kept talking, not realising, not straightaway, that it wasn't impossible. To talk about her flat and for her to no longer be alive.

And then I closed my mouth. Mid-sentence.

I saw his face, and I looked away.

Outside, the evening breeze was lifting the leaves in the courtyard, sending them scuttling across the stone flagging and in through the open door, brushing against our backs as we sat side by side, our knees almost touching, our elbows almost connected, our eyes on the carpet, unable to look at each other.

And as I was about to speak, as I was about to try to tell him I was sorry, I heard the sliding door between our rooms, the glass rattling for a moment and then still.

It was Simon.

Standing there and looking at us.

I moved away, shifting my leg from where it touched Mitchell's, as he, too, moved as he stretched, knees cracking as he pulled himself up from the floor.

All of us speaking at once. Asking Simon to deal. Asking me to move over. Mitchell's voice louder than either of ours as his words crossed over, as he asked Simon where the dope was.

Here, and Simon tossed the bag to him.

Let's go. He turned to Simon. Speaking to him alone. *Take this,* waving the bag in the air, *another bottle, and check out the scenery.*

I watched as Simon started putting on his shoes.

I watched as Mitchell licked the paper flat on a joint.

And I watched as they made their way to the door.

Leaving me alone. Surrounded by cards and piles of matches.

See you. It was Simon who looked back into the room. Just for a moment. Not even long enough for me to say goodbye. And as the front door clicked softly behind them, I was still there, on the floor, next to Mitchell's bed, knowing that I had been left once again, that even if I had attempted to follow, it would have soon been made clear that I was not wanted. That this was different. That I would not be able to rely on Simon's goodwill. That something had changed.

I got up slowly, my head pounding from all we had drunk, and I slid the glass doors between our rooms open. Trying to be quiet. Trying not to wake Evie. Stumbling towards my bed. Closing my eyes and wondering if Mitchell would knock on my door later that night, hoping that he would. Hoping that I hadn't wrecked everything. Whispering my name in the stillness. Just he and I.

Because if he did, I knew I would go out there again. I knew I would follow him out to the step. I knew that I wanted to kiss him. And I wished I hadn't been so stupid. I wished I hadn't kept talking about his mother.

I wished I hadn't upset him.

twenty-seven

Once when I asked Vi why she hated it when people called her a lesbian, she had looked at me, incredulous.

Because I'm not, she had said.

But you live with Mari, you love Mari, you sleep with Mari, I had protested, and she had simply shrugged her shoulders.

So? she had said.

Her ability to shift categories, to place that line wherever she believed it should be and then to justify it with utmost vehemence used to infuriate me.

Now I sometimes find myself envying it.

I wish I could just say: *This is the way it is. This is right and that is wrong.*

But I can't. I just do not know. I stand weighted by the possibilities, the endless justifications that could be used to tip either side of the scales, the infinite definitions that could be given to a single term.

There is no right and there is no wrong.

That is complete and utter rubbish, Vi would tell me, the spark from the end of her cigarette flying out the open window, brilliant for a moment, and then dissolving into ash. *That is what life is all about. Taking the plunge. Drawing the line. You have to,* and she would look at me, fierce, concerned, intense, before being distracted by the telephone ringing somewhere inside the house, or perhaps a knock on the door, or a note she suddenly remembers that she wants to write.

This is the way Vi lives her life. She marks up her territories and she refuses to even glance across to the other side once the fence has been put up.

Now as I try to understand her, as I try to come to terms with decisions that I now know she may have made, I am constantly confronted by this fundamental difference in who we are.

I make my choices but I always seem to have one leg still hanging over the other side of the fence, one eye turned back to what I might have done, what could have been, a cloud of possibilities trailing, twisting, behind me. I think of the decision I made just before the funeral and I have to stop before I am lost in the myriad of options I could have taken, maybe should have taken.

I am different from Vi.

I cannot look back and feel certain. I cannot even define what has passed and is unchangeable. I cannot say, *That is what it was.* I am filled with doubts. Perhaps it was something else, perhaps it could be defined in another way?

Do you think about him often? Simon had asked me.

And I had told him I did.

Sometimes. And then months would pass before he slipped,

stealthy, sure, into my consciousness.

I stood by the window of my flat and found myself trying to say his name out loud. *Mitchell Jenkins.*

The long grass twisting up around his calves, arms folded across his chest, looking out towards the dusty road and then back to me, daring me to follow him, challenging me to jump down and run after him.

He had killed himself.

Mitchell Jenkins killed himself.

I watched myself form the words, my reflection in the window mouthing each syllable, salt smeared across the glass so that my face was cloudy, indiscernible, as I tried to gauge what that sentence actually meant to me.

And I didn't know.

I just didn't know.

I once told Marco about Mitchell. Years ago. We were swapping stories. First loves. Remembering the twists and curls of my stomach, small tendrils of delight, when he had looked at me. Remembering the slow brush of his hand along my leg. Remembering this and not the rest.

Because I had made up a new Mitchell.

I had made up someone whose only place in my life was one of smoky kisses in the darkness.

I watched, sitting high on the cement wall that bordered the verandah, the red paint chipped and flaking beneath my bare feet, shading my eyes from the glare of the morning sun, as Simon carved out Evie's path.

And again, she screamed, as he ran from one end of the

garden to the other, with her perched precariously on his shoulders. *And again.*

And he did.

Cutting his way through the grass. Flattening it as he had flattened it the day before, as he had promised he would do again the next day.

They had left their cereal bowls behind them on the steps. The remains were already curling brown at the edges, drying into the milk under the intensity of the glare. I looked down at them.

I knew that Mitchell was standing behind me. There at the door, shading his eyes with his hands as he, too, looked out, watching them both. And if I turned around I knew that I would see him, his body still wrapped in the warmth of sleep, his hair tousled about his face.

He had not knocked on my door the night before. He had not called me out in the darkness.

And now, in the morning light, I did not turn around to look at him. I just stayed where I was, while Simon and Evie made their way back up to the house, squinting in the sparkle of the dew, Evie sliding down from Simon's shoulders and hitting the ground with a thump.

It got me, she cried, clutching her leg, *the snake.*

And she staggered across the verandah, finally collapsing into a heap, last gasps of air, and then still.

Well, and Mitchell grinned, *looks like we're going to have to bury her,* and he winked at Simon as he took her legs.

Seems like it, and Simon took her arms, the pair of them carrying her limp, back down the stairs and out towards the cool green of the cypress trees.

There in the distance, Evie kicking and squealing in their hold, twisting and turning until she made her way loose and ran back down her path, back towards me, laughing and screaming, unaware that they weren't following her after all.

Collapsing exhausted at my feet.

While Simon and Mitchell slowly walked towards us, standing for a moment to feel the breeze, the direction of the wind, as they consulted each other.

It'd be onshore, and Simon licked the tip of his finger and held it up. *Anyway, doubt whether she'd let us have the car again.*

So what do we do? Mitchell asked, the disappointment clear on his face. He had wanted to have another go. To get up on the board this time. He was certain he could do it. And now there was only the prospect of a whole day here in this place, all this space, stretching in front of him.

It was Evie who wanted to play hide and seek.

Tugging at our arms, *Please, please,* until, unable to bear it any longer, we promised. Just one game.

Sardines? she asked.

And it was Mitchell who was it. Who had to hide, somewhere in the dark rooms of the house, while we looked for him.

Simon, Evie and I with our faces pressed against the corridor wall, the wallpaper peeling in strips, breathing in the powdery dust of the plaster as we counted. Slowly. From one to one hundred.

What now? I asked, forgetting the rules of the game.

Simon explained. Separate and find him. If you find him, hide with him.

And we did.

I went to the back of the house. To the cool of the laundry with its heavy sinks and rusted taps. If I turned them on, the plumbing would groan, letting out a slow trickle of brown, the smell of rusted iron, before it gradually ran clear. Large cupboards with empty shelves that had once held linen, and a cement floor painted dark green, cold through the soles of my sandshoes.

The window looked out onto a stone yard and rusted Hills hoist, and I stood there for a moment, staring at the weeds that grew sticky and wild at the edges. From behind me, I could hear Evie in the kitchen, calling his name, *Mitchell, Mitchell,* opening and closing doors.

Nothing.

Breakfast dishes left on the table, crumbs on the floor and the constant hum of the refrigerator. Behind the door, old wooden brooms and a mop, dry and bedraggled. It was a room with nowhere to hide.

The corridors in that house were dark. Long and wide with a worn strip of carpet that ran down the middle. An old oak sideboard that had rotted on one side, and when I pulled at the front it came off in my hands, clattering to the floor.

I listened.

No sound of the others. And I wondered whether I was the only one left, whether I would open a door and find them all, huddled in the corner. Hidden.

But I didn't. I found Simon. Standing in the middle of their room, looking around him. And he started as I opened the door, letting go of the blind cord so that it swung, too fast, flapping as it hit the top of the frame. Dust dancing in front of our eyes.

Doesn't look like he's in here, Simon said, both of us staring at the unmade beds and mess of clothes.

And I was about to go, to get to the next room before either he or Evie did, when I saw it. A scrap of paper on the floor. Torn from a book. I bent down and picked it up, holding it in both hands as I tilted it under the light. It was a drawing of Mitchell, lying back on his bed, eyes closed, face relaxed.

I was surprised when Simon snatched it from my hands. I was even more surprised when he snapped at me.

You shouldn't just take things, and his face was flushed.

Sensitive or what? and as I glared at him, he folded the drawing up and put it in his bag.

You just shouldn't, and he slammed the door behind him, the handle rattling, loose, precarious, before hitting the floor with a clatter.

I don't know why I thought of the verandah. Probably because the three of us had just assumed that it was out of bounds. I waited until I was sure Evie and Simon were at the other end of the house before I opened the front door, softly, quietly, not wanting to make a sound, just a few inches, not wanting the light to flood down the darkness of the hall, not wanting them to know where I had gone.

It was bright outside.

Glaring white.

And I was, for just a moment, unsteady, unsure, standing there and holding onto the door, not wanting it to slam shut behind me, but not yet able to close it. Waiting for my eyes to adjust.

It was his voice that I heard.

167

Hissing my name.

And I followed.

Round to the side of the house.

He was in a cupboard. A cupboard that had once belonged inside but had been carried out there by some person some time ago. The door was open an inch, and I could see his face. The white of his hair, the gleam of his teeth.

Where are the others?

I told him I didn't know, and he told me he was glad. He had been hoping I would find him.

He stepped out, cobwebs clinging to his shoulders, dust falling from his hair and onto his face. I was about to tell him that he wasn't meant to come out, I was supposed to hide with him, when he leapt over the wall and down onto the grass below.

Staring up at me.

Let's go, he whispered.

And I followed. Running after him, chasing him through the long grass, catching up with him at the gate that separated the garden from all that surrounded us.

I remember. Seeing him standing there. In his jeans and thongs, checked western shirt, arms folded, daring me to follow him. I saw the packet of Winfields tucked into his back pocket and I saw his stride, long and sure, as I ran after him, following him down the dusty, dirt road.

I don't know who led the way. I can only presume it was me. I had, after all, been there before. Through the barbed wire and across the paddock to where the creek wound its way through the hills.

It was still and it was hot. There was no sound except the trickle of the water over the rocks, no shade except the patches beneath the willows.

I watched as Mitchell lit a cigarette, picking a fleck of tobacco off his tongue before passing it to me.

So, we going in? And he lifted his shirt off, over his head, arms high to the sky. He took his jeans off, peeling them down his legs, standing there in front of me with just his underpants on. Nothing else. And he stepped out slowly, unsteady on the rocks beneath his feet, the water swirling brown and cool at his ankles, his knees, just above his thighs, before he slowly sank down, submerging himself for just a moment, shaking his hair as he emerged, a great sparkling spray that seemed to arc out across the water, suspended for an instant, before raining down on me.

And I put the cigarette out.

It is strange what I remember. Wishing Vi had let me buy a bra. Standing there in my underpants and T-shirt, hesitant, unsure as to whether I should take it off or just go in as I was.

I was awkward.

With my T-shirt still on, I made my way out to where he waited, the rocks bruising the soles of my feet. His hand was held out towards me, but I did not take it. I sank down next to him, seeing the white of his skin under water, ghostly pale.

This is tops, and he lay back with his head against a boulder, staring up at the emptiness of the sky, looking, for a moment, like the picture that Simon had drawn.

You know, he said, *I've never been in a river. Till now. Never been in the sea either. Till yesterday,* and he waved his arm through the air. *Reckon I could live here. No worries.*

Don't you think you'd get bored? I asked him.

And he pulled himself up again, standing there in front of me, thinking. *Maybe. Guess you just get used to things. You don't miss what you haven't got.*

He looked down to where the creek disappeared around a bend, staring past me as he spoke, as he asked me what I thought they were trying to do.

I did not know what he meant.

The department. Sending me away with you lot.

I did not know what to say. I shrugged my shoulders.

But I liked it. You know, the other night. When we were out there on those steps.

I turned to him but he wasn't looking at me. He was making his way back to the bank. Stepping up onto a rock near the edge. And I watched as he rolled a joint, his feet still dipped in the creek, yellow leaves caught between his toes, as I made my way over towards him, wanting to tell him that I was sorry for going on about his mother, for asking him questions, but still I didn't say it, afraid that my words would spoil everything.

It's been good you coming, and as I spoke I could not meet his eyes. *You know,* I pointed to the bag of dope and the packet of cigarettes, *you've taught me a few things.*

True.

And he touched my thigh with his finger. It was damp and cool. The flare of the match as he lit the end and leant towards me. The grin on his face as he asked me if I wanted to learn something else. *Ever done a shottie?*

The lit end of the joint in his mouth, the other in mine. My head reeling as I took it in. Wanting to choke. Stopping myself.

I don't know if I kissed him first. When I try to remember, I just don't know. I guess it doesn't matter. Because it was, at first, how I had imagined it would be. The slow rush of the branches in the creek, the warmth of the rock beneath my back, the smooth slide of his hand up my leg, closing my eyes because if I kept them open, it all reeled, too bright, in front of me.

But when I try to remember I just don't know where the dividing line was, or if there was one at all. I can't separate what I wanted from what I didn't want. I could feel my underpants, sliding, wet, down my legs, I could feel him pressed tight against me, and I suppose there was a moment when I tried to push him away, but I am just not sure. His mouth on mine, his hand there, inside me, and then it wasn't his hand. And I could not cry out because he was still kissing me, but I wanted to, I wanted to scream. Watching my fingernails dig into the palm of my hand, not wanting to look at him, not knowing if this was what I wanted, not even knowing what it was that was happening.

Until afterwards.

And when I tried to move, I wanted to be sick. I remember. The slow thickening of nausea, before I hunched forward and vomited in the creek.

twenty-eight

Bernard always calls Mari that old bull dyke.

I have told him several times that this is an offensive term to use. He just smiles. *Of course it is. I wouldn't use it if it wasn't.*

But despite what he calls her, Bernard does have a grudging respect for Mari. Like him, she is a pragmatist. She is aware that there is a right and a wrong, but she is also aware of how irrelevant these concepts can be in striking a path through day to day life.

This is not all they have in common.

Like Bernard, Mari is a person of action. She makes a decision and she immediately tackles all that is necessary to put it into place.

Since my mother has become ill, Mari has turned to me, demanding my involvement in the decisions she implements in order to take charge of the situation.

Shortly after suggesting a family outing, she calls.

You're right, she says. *Vi does need something to occupy her. To take her mind off the fact that she isn't working.*

When I had picked up the phone, I had only been back from work for a few minutes. Tired and fed up, I found it difficult to hide the irritation in my voice. It didn't matter. Mari was oblivious. Wasting very little time on saying hello, she went straight to the point, telling me she would like us all to go on a picnic this weekend. *To the mountains.*

To the mountains?

And I would have assumed that my repetition of her words would have indicated my hesitation about this idea. But she did not seem to notice.

She told me she would organise everything. *Of course.*

I asked her if Simon had agreed to come and she admitted she had not yet put the plan to him. But she was sure he would be there. *It's not like he ever has any arrangements,* she said.

I know I have no choice but to agree. If I don't, I will have to hear the disappointment in her voice. I will have to wear the guilt. But I am also aware that there is an unspoken agenda behind Mari's plan.

Mari has always wanted to move out of the city. She wants dogs, a big garden, and sometimes I get the sneaking suspicion she wants my mother all to herself. She has fantasised about living in the mountains for years, but knowing it would be impossible to manoeuvre Vi into doing something she does not want, she has never really taken any serious steps towards proposing the move.

But things are different now.

Vi is ill and Mari has had to take charge.

And I am anxious that she will try to open up the topic, clearing the way to bring me on side so that I can help influence Vi when she puts the proposal to her.

But she doesn't.

She asks me if I have spoken to Simon recently and I tell her that I haven't.

You know he's been taking time off work?

I didn't and I am surprised. Simon never takes holidays. As far as I know, he has never even taken a sick day.

She says he has had three days off in the last week. *He just walks. I don't know where. But he leaves in the morning, doesn't take his car, and doesn't get home until the early evening.*

Is he all right? There is anxiety in my voice.

I don't think so, she says.

And there is a moment's silence between us before she speaks again. I can tell she is apprehensive, but being the person she is, she wants to tackle the problem, she doesn't want to stay silent any longer.

Did anything happen? she asks me. *At the funeral?*

I have not shut my front door properly and I can hear Mouse coming down the stairs. His footsteps on the path. Slow and heavy. I look down before he passes. But I am too late. He catches my eye and waves, thinking, as he seems to think these days, that there is now some friendship between us.

No, I tell her.

She knows I am lying and she sighs in exasperation.

Ursula, she says. *This is ridiculous. You have no reason not to trust me. If something has happened, and it seems like it has, you should tell me. It's better if we tackle it together, rather than wait for it to burst out and distress your mother. For Christ's sake. I could be a help.*

I do not know what to say.

In the face of her directness, I am left speechless.

I am sorry, I tell her. *It's not that I don't trust you.*

Well, that's certainly the way it seems.

I can't tell you, I say.

And I can't. Worse, the reasons are so complicated that I cannot even attempt to explain them. But I do know that one of the causes of my silence is the fact that I do not want her to have to share my knowledge. I do not want her to have to live with Vi and not know whether Vi knows what I have recently learnt, and, if so, what that means. Or whether she should tell her.

She sighs again in frustration.

Think about it, she says. *If you change your mind, I am ready to listen.*

I know, I tell her and I hope she can detect the fact that I am trying from the tone of my voice.

So, she says. *You will come on Sunday?*

And I promise her I will.

twenty-nine

Vi always told me that it would be a shame to lose my virginity too young. She told me she disagreed with people who believed there was no significance attached to the occasion.

It's not that I ascribe to any form of puritanical morality, she would say. *But nor do I believe that sex should be taken lightly.*

She would tell me that I should be certain. I should be sure that it was what I wanted. I should be able to trust without fear.

I was sixteen when she gave me those talks. No doubt the timing was influenced by her work of the moment. She was sitting on a government committee into the rights of the child. They were examining, among other issues, the age of consent.

I would be on my way out and she would suddenly call me back. She would shift her papers to one side, light a cigarette and tell me to sit down. She would lean forward and reach for my hands. I would find it impossible to meet the intensity of her gaze. She would tell me that I shouldn't be afraid of talking to her; if I was confused or unsure, talking could help.

I would look at her as though I didn't understand. Although

I did. Perfectly. And I would tell her I was just going out. With friends. Girlfriends.

I just wanted you to know, she would say, *that I'm here.*

Sure, and I would shrug my shoulders, without meeting her gaze.

The talk would be over and she would tell me to have a good time, never knowing that she was too late. Two years too late.

But she was not the only one to whom I lied.

I didn't tell my friends either.

I pretended to be like them, face to face with a hurdle that was soon to be surmounted. And, at sixteen and a half, when I had sex with Matthew Cale in his parents' bedroom, I marked that occasion as the first. He was as inexperienced as I pretended to be, and I doubt whether he ever knew the truth of the matter. I am sure that none of my friends did. They had no reason to suspect.

But that was not how I lost my virginity. When it happened, I was not drunk. I was not at a party, slipping away into another room, pretending to be unaware of the knowing looks that shot backwards and forwards as we closed the door behind us. Confronted with his mother's pear-shaped bed, we fell down on the satin bedspread, fumbling with each other's clothes.

Do you want to? Matthew had whispered into my ear.

Sure, I had said, seeing no reason not to, particularly in light of the fact that it was, after all, nothing new.

And, not wanting to remember Mitchell, I came to think of that drunken fumble as the first. Until I found that I had forgotten what had happened two years earlier. And when I did remember, when it darted, bent low and quick, into my consciousness, I would flinch, pushing it aside as rapidly as it had appeared.

I did not tell Simon what happened by the creek.

Just as I remember walking back from the rocks with Anton and seeing them, Marco and Louise, watching us as we climbed up the cliff path, both of us acting as though nothing had happened, I remember seeing Simon on the verandah, watching us as Mitchell and I came towards him.

We had crossed the paddock without a word, shading our eyes from the glare of the sun, brushing at the flies with the backs of our hands, until we reached the barbed-wire fence.

I could feel the sweat trickling down my back, and my T-shirt clinging to my skin, clammy and warm, as Mitchell lifted the fence to let me through.

I did not look at him and he did not look at me.

You okay? he asked and it was all he said. The only words spoken in what seemed to be a journey of interminable silence punctuated only by the sound of the gravel beneath our feet, loud in the stillness that surrounded us.

He was on one side of the road and I was on the other. I ached between my thighs, but I did not want to look down, I did not want to see my legs moving as they had always moved, so I looked out, across the sweep of the paddocks gently rising, smooth and dusky, towards the hills.

He lit another cigarette and I heard the strike of the flint. As he tossed the match across the road, we glanced at each other, for just a moment.

The sharpness of his face beneath the high blue sky.

And we walked on in silence.

I do not know whether Mitchell was aware that Simon had sketched him, or whether Simon had tried to capture his profile in secret, furtively, stealing glances as Mitchell slept. The straight line of his nose, the wide mouth, the curve of his cheek, hair like straw hanging into his eyes. All of this.

I had held the drawing in my hands and Simon had snatched it from me.

And when I had looked at my brother's face I had seen shame, and embarrassment.

As we walked back, I, too, felt shame and embarrassment, but for different reasons. I did not want to look at Mitchell. I did not want to see, there, next to me, his face. A face that I, too, had stolen glances at, a face that I had conjured up before I went to sleep, painting in each feature, slowly, carefully.

A face that was now too familiar.

When I look back on that day now, I still feel shame as I remember. Shame that is confused with his death, but shame nonetheless.

The white gate was ahead of us. Hanging from its one hinge, lopsided in the thick grass. The dark cypress trees, the old well, and beyond them the red roof of the house, those colours like beacons in the distance as we made our way slowly along the last stretch of that road, without a word.

Later, when Vi would try to tell me that it would be a pity to lose my virginity too young, I would, for a brief instant, remember that walk. The heat, the stillness and the silence. The vastness around us. The dryness in my mouth, the taste of having been sick. She would speak and I would want to tell her she was too late. But I would keep my silence.

When I tried to lift the gate, when I tried to pull it up from where it scraped through the grass, cutting ruts into the green, I found I had no strength.

It was Mitchell who had to let us in. It was Mitchell who led the way, across the garden to where Simon waited for us on the verandah steps.

And I followed, head down, three steps behind, to where he sat, there on the top step, knees drawn up near his chest, watching us.

Watching us and saying nothing.

Simon has dark eyes. Dark like mine. Dark like Vi's. Dark like Evie's. But different.

The eyes of an innocent, Mari has said and not in affection, but usually in annoyance as Simon sits unaware of her frustration with his stillness, confused by her sudden bursts of anger when he has, once again, failed to *pull his weight.*

Where have you been?

It was Mitchell who told him.

We'd been to the creek. Had a swim. The ordinariness of his words hanging in the stillness.

A fly buzzed near my mouth and I brushed it away.

An ant crawled, slowly, up my shin.

You should have told me, and Simon scratched the side of his arm, awkward, uncertain as to what had happened, unsure as to where he stood.

I tried to look at him. Evie's joke book was open, dog-eared by his side, a glass of water sweating in the heat, a plate with the remains of a sandwich, all of this, and him.

I looked. His words were hesitant. *Everywhere.*

And standing out there with the sun beating down on my head, on my shoulders, with that taste in my mouth, and with the ache in my legs, I tried to say I was sorry but I was surprised to find that I had no words. An open mouth and not a thing to say.

So it was Mitchell who apologised. It was Mitchell who told him we had meant to come back earlier. It was Mitchell who said that time had just got away. Slipped away. *You know how it is.*

Reckon, I said, finally finding a word, any word, a word that was not my word.

Anyway, we're back, Mitchell said.

We are, I repeated.

And I bent down to do up my shoelace, to try to find a way of sliding away from the hurt in my brother's eyes, but my fingers didn't seem to work.

I needed to get inside.

I needed to be alone.

I remember.

I let Mitchell keep talking as I pushed my way past Simon, wanting to get into the house, wanting to get into the cool, wanting to be by myself, just for a little while.

And I didn't say anything to him.

I didn't even look at him.

The door swung shut behind me and I left them, Simon and Mitchell, out there on the verandah.

thirty

It is Lizzie who takes me to have the termination.

When I mentioned I had booked the clinic, she had insisted on taking me.

Don't, she had said when I had protested, when I had told her I was happy to go on my own. *Let go of the stupid bravado. Just for once.*

She is, as always, calm and sensible. She reassures me that I am doing the right thing, that the situation is impossible, that there is, really, no choice.

But I am still uncertain, I am still battling with the decision as we cross through the back streets of the city, Lizzie driving as she always drives, too fast, swearing loudly at other drivers, beeping her horn at every car that is slow off the mark.

I hold onto the dashboard and close my eyes.

Her driving is the only chink in her calm persona. She once told me it was because her father died in a car crash, and she has felt a need to defy his death ever since.

I tell her I am scared I will regret my choice, that I have made it when I have had too many other matters on my mind (although I do not tell her what these other matters are; I cannot bring myself to talk of Mitchell).

She tells me I have to trust myself. I have to have faith in my own decision-making capabilities.

I tell her I am worried I will never meet anyone else, worried I will never be pregnant again.

She tells me not to be silly. *Look at me,* she says. *All those years on my own and I've found someone.*

I tell her that I wanted to have a child while Vi was still alive, and I am looking out the window as I speak, not trusting myself to keep from crying, as she tells me that I cannot do something as momentous as this for my mother.

Besides, she says, *there's no reason why Vi won't live for a lot longer. The doctors have told you that,* and she reaches for my hand, swerving dangerously as she does so.

And I tell her what the doctor told me, that I may have problems conceiving, that I had tried earlier and nothing had happened, that perhaps this is my only chance, that perhaps I am being a fool.

She is about to reassure me once again, but then she changes her mind. She pulls over, the car skidding on the dirt beside the road.

With the ignition turned off, I can hear the wind in the Moreton Bay figs, stirring the last leaves, and I watch as they fall to the ground, to the roots, knotted like elephant hide at the base of the trunk.

They all have a disease, I said.

And she looks at me. She does not know what I am talking about.

These trees. All of them. They're all losing their leaves. And they don't know what it is.

She switches off the radio.

I ask her if there's any trick she's learnt in meditation that helps you make up your mind in a situation like this.

She tells me that ever since she rediscovered sex, she's forgotten it all, and even if she could remember, she doesn't think it was ever a question of tricks. Unfortunately.

What a shame, I say.

You know you don't have to do this, and she looks at me. *It's not too late to change your mind.*

I know.

I just needed to say all my doubts out loud. I just needed to put them on the table. I suppose I hoped that if I voiced them, they would vanish. Each one lined up, examined and put to rest, buried deep, deep enough to be forgotten.

But that is not how it is. And I have to remember why I made my decision. I have to remember what it would mean to have a child and to keep silent as Anton has asked me to do, or to tell and face what that would incur; to be alone with a baby, to have a baby in those circumstances. I would not have the strength. I could not do it.

You know, Lizzie says, *you'll probably hate me for saying this.*

Then don't say it, I tell her.

But it's a pity it wasn't Marco.

And I tell her that I do hate her for saying it, that she shouldn't have, and I am about to get out of the car. I am

184

about to slam the door behind me and walk to the clinic, but she stops me.

Do you want to do this? she asks me.

No, I say.

And she turns the key in the ignition. She knows that I have made up my mind. That I do not want to do it, but I will do it. She knows what I meant when I said no, and she squeezes my hand as we pull back onto the road.

We're late, I say.

And she puts her foot on the accelerator.

thirty-one

It was cool on the morning of the funeral, and when I opened the front door to my flat and smelt the salt in the freshness of the air, I remembered what winter was like. The chill as the wind whistles through the gap between the door and the wall, the fog at night, the crisp clarity of the days; I remembered and I shivered.

These were the mornings when I would get up and tell Marco that there were not many swimming days left for the summer.

Probably more than you think, he would say, trying to keep me in bed.

I would ignore him, feeling the change in the air as I pulled on my swimmers and wrapped my towel around my shoulders.

The ocean was still rough.

A great rolling swell that had the surfers up and out the back, black flecks against the morning sky.

The pool was also wild. The waves slapped the sides, backwards, forwards, rolling over the cracked cement, sparkling, frosty green, icy as they surged against each other, pushing and pulling me from wall to wall.

Standing under the shower, I washed seaweed from my body, slippery greens and browns, mossy and soft beneath my fingers, tiny red welts across my stomach from the end of a stinger's tail, and sand between my toes. The steam rose and I let it all slide off me.

Bernard had called the night before, telling me to ring him as soon as I got back. To let him know what had happened.

Mari had also called, reminding me to look after Simon.

I had listened but I had not really listened. I had held the phone away from my ear while they spoke.

Promise, Bernard had said.

Promise, Mari had said.

And I had promised them both.

Anton had also called, his voice a whisper as he left a message. I could hear him there above me, the scrape of his chair along the floor as he moved closer to the phone, and I could only guess that Louise was also there upstairs, somewhere out of hearing.

He had told me he wanted to talk. He had messed it all up. But he was not deserting me. He promised. And I had turned the volume down on his words. I had wiped his message as soon as he left it.

Standing by my rack of clothes and flicking through everything I owned, I saw all the different stages of myself on lurid display.

Like Vi, I am a secret and compulsive shopper, but where Vi will buy hundreds of pairs of high-heeled shoes, cardigans, pastel skirts and blouses, each one almost identical to the last, I buy a constantly changing array of new looks.

I once told Lizzie that I thought I would be able to mount a solo exhibition of every tragic fashion foisted on women in the last two decades. She hadn't argued with me.

Photographs of your haircuts alone would be enough, she had said.

I had grimaced with embarrassment.

I chose a skirt I would wear to work and then put it back, remembering that I did not intend to get out of the car. My jeans and a T-shirt were lying on the floor and I picked them up and held them in front of me for a moment before I decided to put them on. I wished I also had a pair of thongs.

Simon was punctual, as always.

If he felt any dismay at the way I was dressed, he said nothing.

His jeans were new, dark blue, stiff like cardboard and straining at the waist. His shirt was also new, maroon and, like his pants, too small. As I opened the door to him, I realised it had been a long time since I had seen him in anything but his bus driver's uniform. The clothes he wore outside work were not all that different.

Shall we go? and he looked at me anxiously, wanting me to be ready.

I told him to wait for me up on the road. I promised him I wouldn't be long.

But he didn't.

I could see him out on the path, smoking one of the cigarettes from his never-ending supply and kicking the toe of his shoe through the sand and dirt that had slipped down in the last storms.

It has been so many years since Simon and I have been able to speak to each other. Since Candelo. But before then, it was different. I was always there, tagging along, wanting his attention, wanting to be part of his older and seemingly more impressive world.

Whereas Simon was just Simon. Never really with me. Never really with anyone. Just complete within himself.

And although I knew this, I didn't give up.

I would set up camp down by the waterfront, smuggling food and blankets down there, stashing them in a cave. I would try to convince him to run away with me, to hide, to make Vi worried. I could see it made no sense to him. But through sheer insistence, I would make him follow, both of us riding our skateboards down the steep hill that led to the reserve.

Within an hour we would be bored.

I would try to entertain him. I would want to keep him there with me. I would pretend we had no food. That we were starving. I would scramble over outcrops of sandstone, cutting my knees and feet as I scraped oyster shells off the surface of the rocks, eating them in front of him, urging him to eat with me. I would make us a fishing pole from bamboo. I would make up stories about children who had survived for months on their own without anyone to look after them. *True,* I would say.

Nothing ever worked.

Within a couple of hours, he would tell me that he was going.

He would make me promise to come home before it got dark.

And then he would leave me alone.

Still, I didn't give up.

I would follow him after school, hanging with his friends, wanting to be where he was, even though it would be clear that despite Simon's tolerance, the others did not want me around.

Boys only, Steven Cobden would say.

Oh yeah? I would challenge him, with my hands on my hips, daring him to make me go.

Yeah, and he would take one step closer.

Says who? I would ask, wanting to keep him there at bay, hoping that Simon would eventually notice what was going on, hoping that he would intervene on my behalf.

But he never had any idea. He just kept doing whatever it was he happened to be doing. And I would march home, furious, let down, while he remained completely unaware of the indignity I had suffered.

I had wanted it to be reversed. I had wanted the tables to be turned. I had wanted Simon to want me, to follow me, to chase me. And I had wanted to be like him. Oblivious.

As he stubbed out his cigarette in the garden and told me we had to get going, we were running late, I remembered this and I thought about what it was like now. Different. But the same.

Because when I saw him, completely closed down, completely locked up, I knew he was further from me than ever, and it still had me. Only now I was just trying to fix it. To make it better. Still knowing that I never would, that he would always be somewhere else. And·as I followed him up the path to the road without saying a word, I thought about the strangeness of this day. The fact that he had asked me for something. To help him. That it was, perhaps, the first time this had happened.

When we reached the top he was out of breath and wiping the sweat from his forehead.

His car was a mess and I opened my window wide, trying to find an escape from the stale smell of the overflowing ashtray.

He pushed the street directory towards me and told me where it was we were going.

Can you direct? he asked.

I told him I felt sick if I had to look at a map.

He didn't reply and I turned to the page he had marked.

It's miles away, I said.

He turned the key in the ignition. *I know. That's why I didn't want to be late.*

Simon drives a car like he drives a bus. Both hands firmly on the steering wheel, each turn is exaggerated, too large. He drives slowly, sitting firmly in the middle of the lane, always braking in plenty of time, never losing his temper, never taking a risk.

Are you nervous? I asked him and because he did not answer me, I turned to the window, letting the cool breeze rush across my cheeks. It was colder than it had been for months and I wished I had brought a jumper with me.

I turned on the radio and twisted the dial until I found a station without too much static.

What's happened to the aerial? I asked him.

191

He told me he had never had one.

Hits and memories. A classic from the seventies. And as I found myself humming in tune to a song that we had once both liked, I looked across at him, but he did not turn towards me.

When he finally told me that he was *a bit anxious,* I had forgotten my question. It took me a moment to realise that he was responding, and in that moment, it was too late. He had looked away again.

As we pulled up at the traffic lights, he lit another cigarette. I took one from his pack.

I thought you didn't smoke, and he looked at me, genuinely perplexed, as he passed me the lighter. It glowed, bright orange, one burning fleck of tobacco stuck to the coils.

I don't, I lied. *Not often,* and as I drew back I felt the smoke scratch the back of my throat.

As the news came on the radio, Simon turned it off.

Why did you do that? I asked him.

I don't like it. I don't like hearing those things, and he changed down gears, slowly, methodically, leaving plenty of space between us and the truck in front.

It's just the news. I went to turn it on again, expecting him to lean forward and stop me, but he didn't.

A young girl had been burnt to death. Doused in kerosene and burnt. The man was in police custody. The truck in front inched forward. There were floods in Poland. Fifteen dead. We also moved forward. Simon kept his eyes on the road.

Did you stay in touch with him? I, too, was staring straight in front. I did not look at my brother but I could see his reflection in the windshield. He knew that I was referring to Mitchell. His name was unspoken but it hung there, between us.

I saw him nod.

I wrote to him.

I looked at his hands on the gearstick. Long, fine fingers. Out of place with the rest of his body. Hands that had belonged to the old Simon, tall, slim and graceful on the steps at Candelo, stretching in the morning sun.

He never wrote back.

I kept my eyes on him, there in the glass, his face washed out, watered-down planes of colour marking cheeks, eyes, nose, mouth.

I even tried to visit him once. In the institution.

His cigarette glowed as he drew back, and for a moment the smoke clouded his face. *He wouldn't see me,* and as we swung onto the freeway, away from the sun, his reflection disappeared, wiped out, just the smears on the windscreen left in its place.

I flicked my butt onto the road and watched the sparks fly behind us. There in the rear-vision mirror, dancing orange, flying backwards.

Left at the next lights, I told him and he nodded.

I wound up my window, trying to drown out the wind rushing, the other cars, waiting for Simon to speak again and knowing that if I pushed him, he would stop. So I stayed silent.

He told me he had tried to find Mitchell when he had got out.

How? I asked him, not wanting to look surprised.

We braked slowly and I listened to the slow grind of the truck in front of us.

You know, phone book.

He had tried to find his mother first. He had forgotten she was dead. And as he told me this, I looked across at him wondering whether he remembered how I had refused to believe Mitchell when he had told us this.

He had searched for his sister next.

I remembered Mitchell telling me she managed a shop. I wondered whether he had also told Simon. I wondered how close they had been.

He was in jail again. Simon's words were slow and hesitant. Armed robbery. Twenty years.

The trees near the side of the road were swaying in the breeze. Tall palms, bending delicately, arcing through the sky. I watched them as Simon told me how he had tried again. Writing to him, his letters returned unanswered. Driving out to visit him, driving home again.

He had never said. He had never told any of us. For all that time.

Why?

He didn't answer.

He wiped the sweat from his forehead.

He asked me where the next turn-off was.

I tried to look down at the map, the tangle of roads a blur in front of me, the smell from the ashtray rising in the stillness of the car.

Can you pull over? I asked him, and he looked at me. Just for a moment.

Now?

I could feel the nausea rising, from my stomach to my

throat, my head light, swallowing it back, until Simon came to a halt, and by the side of the road, next to the curb, I hunched forward and vomited.

Dry weeds, cans and cigarette butts.

Each one slowly coming back into focus as Simon moved across to the passenger seat and passed me his handkerchief. It was clean, freshly ironed, and I did not know what to do with it.

He leant forward and wiped my forehead, and the gentleness of his touch surprised me.

It's okay, and I sat in the gutter while he waited anxiously in the front seat. *Just carsick.*

He looked at his watch.

We've got to get going, and his voice was apologetic.

I stood up slowly, my legs unsteady, and got back in.

I need a drink, I said, and he nodded his head. *To get rid of the taste.*

He passed me a bottle of Coke, warm and flat, and studied the map.

Sorry, I said. *It always happens.*

He closed the directory and started the car.

Not far now, and as he pulled out onto the road again, I shut my eyes and tried to understand what it was he had been saying.

thirty-two

Why is it called Candelo? I asked Vi when we first arrived, the name of the town illuminated for just a moment by the headlights of the car.

We were driving down the deserted main street. Two streetlights. Everything closed. Mitchell, Evie and I in the back seat, Simon in the front. Mitchell with the instructions on his lap, directing us to the house.

In the darkness it was difficult to see anything. It was difficult to know where we were. The shadow of the hills on either side of us and to our left the sound of the river rushing.

Through the dust that caked the car window, I could see the name of the town written on the buildings, Candelo General Store, Candelo Pub, Candelo Post Office, faded white paint on what had once been thriving businesses but were now too large, almost ridiculous in their size.

Vi told me that people used to take this road when they travelled from the north to the south. *It was a journey that took days,* she said.

This was where they arrived when the sun was setting, when night crept in, purple and soft, over the hills.

They were on horseback, she said. *There were no streetlights. They had no torches.*

And as they clattered over the bridge, they called out for light. *Candel-o,* their voices ringing out in the darkness.

Candles to light their way into town, to light their way to warmth, a bed for the night.

Candles to light their way on to the next part of the journey, so that they could see what was out there, so that they could see what was real and what was not.

And what was true and what was false.

Candelo, and I whispered the word to myself as we drove on in the darkness.

I did not know my brother.

I did not know him then, all those years ago at Candelo, and I do not know him now.

It was Bernard who asked me if I had ever considered the possibility that Simon was *a little in love with Mitchell.* It was Bernard who finally spoke the words out loud.

I was surprised. Not by the suggestion, but by the fact that my father was astute in his observation of his own son's feelings.

We were sitting in his apartment. It was the day after the funeral. And because I was at a loss as to what to do, I had gone to my father for help. For answers. Normally he would have been the least likely source of assistance, but this time he was the only person to whom I could turn.

From his window overlooking the gardens, I could see that

summer was rapidly becoming autumn. Almost overnight. The trees below were losing leaves, some branches already smooth-limbed against the flat sky.

My father lives in an old building. A gracious 1920s apartment block, one of the few in the city. His apartment commands one of the better views, across the sweep of office blocks and parklands and out to the harbour.

Samantha, his girlfriend, was in the process of moving out. There were removalists carrying the last of her possessions across the grand parquetry entrance hall and out to the elevator as we spoke. My father kept his eye on them. Every so often he jumped up mid-sentence and extracted a book or a statuette from an open box as they took it to the door.

She's shameless, he told me as he placed a dark-red Venetian glass decanter on the dining-room table.

I shrugged my shoulders. *Maybe she's angry.*

He looked surprised at the suggestion. *She has no reason to be,* he said.

I could have explained that people get upset when they are thrown over for another, but there was no point. He is what he is and no doubt he will remain the same until the day he dies.

He settled back in his armchair and looked directly at me. The last box had been carried out the door and he could concentrate.

So, he said, and he rubbed at his chin with the palm of his hand. *It seems as though we need to go through this from the beginning.*

From out in the lobby, the elevator clanged shut. The front door was still open and Bernard got up to close it.

I had gone there hoping he would be direct with me.

I had gone there hoping he would explain everything.

But I could see that it was not going to be so easy.

Simon told you he tried to stay in touch with Mitchell? and as he crossed his legs, he revealed the Italian silk socks he likes to wear.

I nodded my head.

He wanted to go through it all slowly, methodically. He did not want the torrent of words that had begun as soon as I had arrived, out of breath, telling him about our drive out to the service, speaking too quickly, perhaps even accusingly, until he had stopped me. Until he had made his comment about Simon being in love with Mitchell.

He was right.

Simon was a little in love. I can see that now and I cannot help but wonder whether I had known it then.

We both were. In our own ways.

And as I looked at my father, I wanted to ask him when he had come to that conclusion. When he had realised, and how. But I didn't.

Unlike Vi, Bernard is a believer in love. *An impossible romantic,* he says and he throws his hands up in the air and laughs loudly.

He turns over girlfriends at a rapid rate, but I have little doubt that he loves each of them, passionately, at the time.

Also unlike Vi, he likes to talk about love, about the personal, about each of my involvements; he likes to advise. He is, after all, somewhat of an expert in the affairs of the heart.

So it has always been him I have told whenever I have fallen in love or out of love. Even though I do not speak to him nearly as often as I speak to Vi. Even though I will go months without seeing him. Even though I have far more in common with my mother.

But I had not come to him on that day to talk about love.

He stood up slowly and asked me if I would like a glass of wine. *It's been a long day,* he said, indicating the mess that had been left behind by the removalists.

I told him I would.

On his sideboard, Bernard has a photograph of Simon and me. It was taken years ago, when he still lived with us. By a photographer who was unknown but is now famous; the reason, I suspect, for the display.

I picked it up and looked at it, holding it under the light, surprised as I always was at the enormity of the change that had occurred in my brother.

I put it down when I heard my father's footsteps across the hall.

So, he said, as he placed his grandfather's silver tray on the table between us. *Simon tried to contact him,* and he passed a glass across to me, *for all those years.*

For all those years.

And as my father took his glasses off and wiped them on the bottom of his shirt, I could not help but feel that I was about to hear him deliver a closing address.

Prepared while he was in the kitchen.

Well modulated and reasoned.

I sipped my wine and I waited for him to begin.

thirty-three

Vi is fierce in her condemnation of Bernard's betrayal of her, and of us.

Never rely on your father for anything, she used to warn us. *I have certainly learnt not to.*

I have never asked my father why he left. I have always just accepted the version of events that we came to understand from Vi. My father was and is a man who constantly runs off with new women. He is a man of little moral fibre. He is a man who betrays. This is how Vi describes him and this is the filter through which I see him. But it does not mean I do not love him. It does not mean there is no other side.

I am heading up the path on my way out to meet a friend for breakfast and thinking about how Vi would define my betrayal, if I ever told her about it, when I walk straight into a removalist.

He asks me if I am Louise and I tell him I am not. She lives in the upstairs flat at the bottom of the stairs.

Are they moving? I ask.

He tells me they are. In a couple of weeks. He is coming to give a quote. *Hell of a job,* he says, and he shakes his head as he looks back up to the street and then down to where the stairs are now almost completely overgrown.

Where to? I ask him.

Interstate, he says. *Company job. Transfer.*

Louise's work, no doubt. The organisation she works for is a national one.

I watch him make his way down the path, and I wonder what it will be like to live here without them and without Marco, without all the betrayals that linked us together, and all the justifications we invented to prop them up.

It is hard to imagine.

And I am surprised that the relief I feel at their departure is tempered by a sadness.

An unexpected emptiness, that I cannot quite explain.

Simon saw what we had done as a betrayal. But it was, perhaps, Mitchell who had hurt him the most. It was Mitchell to whom he had turned for an explanation, Mitchell who was left to do the talking, while I made my way slowly down the long corridor to the bathroom.

We must be careful with water, Vi had warned us when we arrived. *Quick showers,* knowing how Simon and I liked to stand under for hours.

The bath was old, the enamel chipped and stained.

The steam rose, cloudy and sweet with Vi's salts, half the container. Leaves stuck to my stomach, a smear of mud down my thigh, and the beginning of a bruise inside my leg. Mauve, yellow; I traced its outline with the tip of my finger.

And as I lowered myself into the water, I closed my eyes, wanting to block out everything but the sense of being submerged, safe, alone.

In the heat of the afternoon, Evie set up shop. Games, fruit, biscuits, cups and saucers, carried out one by one and displayed along the verandah wall; the prices that Simon had drawn up for her, 5c, 2c, 10c, propped up next to each item.

The clatter of her feet down the hall. Calling out my name: *Ursula, Ursula, come to my shop. Come and buy something.*

Sinking myself further into the water, trying not to hear.

There at Vi's door.

My mother looking up from her typewriter and telling Evie she would come out soon. Very soon.

And in the dim of that bathroom, the steam slowly dissipated until I could see the sharp outlines of my knees, my hands, and, not liking what I saw, I turned on the hot, again and again. Letting it run until the water flowed over the edge of the tub, carrying the soap with it, spilling onto the floor, seeping out under the door, until Vi was there, demanding to know what on earth I was doing.

Nothing, I said, not looking at her.

You're wrinkled like a prune.

And the plumbing groaned as she turned the tap off, and groaned again as I turned it straight back on.

For God's sake, and she plunged her hand in, pulling out the plug before I could stop her. *What is wrong with you?*

I told her I didn't feel well.

She told me not to be so silly.

I shivered as I sat in the now empty tub and she passed me a towel. *Get some clothes on and go and dry your hair in the sun.*

I heard the door slam shut behind her. I heard the silence. And then I heard the sound of her typewriter.

It was the quiet outside that made me go out there.

The front door wide open, the afternoon light slanting in, a honey gold on the walls of that corridor, on the worn carpet and on the dark boards beneath.

It would have been a beautiful garden once. It still was, but overgrown and wild. What had once been a circular drive was now covered with grass. What had once been a well was choked with weeds. And I stood on that verandah and looked out past the cypress trees to where the hills shone, soft and warm under the cloudless sky.

A slight breeze lifted the first of Evie's cardboard signs, black texta on white cardboard. It floated off the verandah and out across the grass, to where it finally rested underneath a twisted lemon tree. I followed the next one, walking barefoot through the garden, as each of her price tags drifted past me, picking them up as I went, 10c, 5c, 2c bundled together in my hand.

No one in sight.

And I looked back at the house, at the strange pile of items on the verandah, at Simon's plate, his sketchbook, at Mitchell's sandshoes, and at my own sandshoes leaning up against his.

In that quiet, the house could have been deserted again. It could have been empty, the way it was when we arrived, the way it would be when we left, and as I made my way back across the garden, one eye on the ground watching for snakes,

I wondered where they had gone. Because I wanted to see him. Mitchell. I wanted to see him and I didn't want to see him. I wanted to know that everything was all right, that there by the river he had loved me and I had loved him, and that it was beautiful. The way it was in stories. The way I was trying to believe that it had happened.

But they were nowhere in sight.

And as I stood there on the top step and looked back behind me one more time, I saw what I had somehow failed to see only a few moments earlier. The car had gone. The grass flattened, yellowing, in the place where it had been parked.

I called out to Vi as I slammed the door shut behind me.

She did not answer.

I could hear her radio as I pushed her door open.

Where are they? I asked.

She did not look up.

Where have they gone?

She was not listening.

With the volume up, with her cigarette in one hand and her gaze turned towards the page in front of her, she had not heard a word I'd said.

But I was insistent. *Have they gone to the beach?* my voice determined as I waited for an answer.

She did not know what I was talking about.

They've taken the car.

And she took off her glasses and put them down on the table next to her, looking at me for the first time.

Of course they haven't, and as she folded her arms, I could see that she was exasperated, that she didn't know what had *got into me.* She turned back to her work and was about to start typing, her fingers poised over the keys, but I stopped her. I took her by the hand and pulled her up after me, tiny without her heels, no taller than I was, and I made her follow me, back up that corridor and out onto the verandah to see. For herself.

It had gone.

And they had gone with it.

With Evie? she asked me.

I told her I didn't know.

She was furious.

Those fucking idiots.

I turned to her in surprise.

Jesus, and she stamped her foot in anger. *I don't know what to do,* the frustration marked on her face.

I looked out to where the road wound its way back towards the town. I looked at her. *We wait, I suppose.*

And that is what we did.

thirty-four

Simon wanted to buy flowers.

We were almost there. On the outskirts of the city where the houses sprawl one after the other, front yards still parched from the summer, cars parked out the front with 'For Sale' signs taped to their windows, garbage cans left out in the gutters from the collection that morning.

I thought we were running late.

Simon checked his watch. There was, he said, just enough time.

We stopped at a corner store, buckets of wilted daisies and roses lined up next to newspaper banners behind wire. I watched as Simon chose the ones he wanted, hesitating as he picked out one bunch and then another.

I think you're meant to send them to the funeral home or something. Not take them with you.

Simon looked anxiously at the flowers in my lap. The paper in which they were wrapped was covered with faded pictures of balloons, pale reds, yellows and greens dancing across a dirty-blue background.

Maybe it's okay, I tried to reassure him. But I didn't really know.

The only funeral I had ever been to was Evie's.

Simon turned the key in the ignition and pulled out slowly, the steering groaning as he tried to turn back to the road we had been on. I held onto the dashboard and closed my eyes. On my lap, the roses were squashed tight together so that the petals appeared closer, the buds younger than they really were. I could feel the thorns through the paper and I put them down on the floor.

There had been roses in Evie's coffin. White ones. I opened the car window wide and stuck my head out, wanting to feel the freshness of the air, as I remembered peering into the casket, wanting to look, but not wanting to.

With the make-up thick on her face and her hair brushed back, she had seemed like a doll. China-pink cheeks. Rose-red lips. And as Vi had leant forward to kiss her, the shroud had slipped slightly and I had seen, for one moment, the white of her feet.

I should have cut her nails. Vi had asked me to, the night before the accident, and I hadn't. She had squirmed out of my grasp in the bath and I had let her go, running up the hall towards Simon, naked and dripping wet. *In the raw.*

Evie was cremated.

Mitchell was going to be buried.

The cemetery stretched across block after block. It was a suburb in itself, with small paths dividing it up, crisscrossing the miles of flat neat land, each one named and marked on the map at the entrance.

Do you know where to go? I asked Simon.

He shook his head.

We sat in the car feeling foolish.

What do we do? I looked at him.

He told me he didn't know.

With the engine idling, we watched as a procession of mourners followed a long, black hearse towards the southern end of the cemetery. Just as I was about to suggest that we go and ask, Simon turned the car in their direction and we moved into the end of the file.

The car park was only a couple of yards from the grave, and as we pulled up next to a dusty red Commodore, I could see that there was no way I was going to be able to stay hidden, sunk low in the passenger seat, until the service was over.

Are you coming? Simon tried to tuck his shirt into his too tight jeans. He brushed his hair back from his face.

This was not what I had wanted.

I could feel a tiny trickle of sweat sliding down my back. My mouth was dry, and my hands unsteady as I tried to undo my seat belt.

As I got out of the car, he offered me a cigarette. I took it and held it unlit between my thumb and forefinger.

They were standing under a gum tree. A small group of mourners, clustered around an open grave. No faces that I knew. No faces that knew us. And as I took my place next to Simon, behind the others, I could smell the freshness of the dirt, rich brown, darker than the dirt beneath my feet, pungent and sweet.

I do not remember what the priest said. With my eyes on the ground, his words floated over me, phrases drifting high into the flat grey of the sky; a strange, disjointed homily. *A troubled life. Peace at last.* Each time I tried to grasp a word, to cling onto the phrase to which it belonged, I would feel it slipping away, sliding like water between my fingers.

This was it.

This was what his life had come to.

This was what I was trying to grasp, my eyes fixed on the ground, but it was not him I was thinking of. It was Evie I kept seeing. Evie on the verandah at Candelo. Evie in that coffin.

I looked down at my hands, one clasping the wrist of the other.

White knuckles.

And as the breeze lifted, a pile of leaves whirled at my feet, dust and grit flying high and falling in one brief moment. There was dirt in my eye and I rubbed at it furiously.

Kerry will now say a few words.

I looked up, my eye still red and sore, as the priest moved aside and a woman of about forty-five took his place. Small and thin with sandy blonde hair, dyed and teased back from a tight drawn face.

And I listened as she spoke, her voice wavering as she said that she knew he had been trouble, but she had still loved him and she was sorry, so sorry, that it had come to this. *Oh, Jesus,* and she blew her nose. *He was my brother, the only family I had, and I will miss him.*

The man in front of me shifted awkwardly, the single rose in his hand wilting, the petals brown at the tips. And as he stepped forward to throw the flower into the grave, I tried to catch Simon's eye, because I did not want to stay here any longer. I did not want to be a part of this. This was not our mourning. This was not anything to do with us.

And I was alarmed at the bitterness still in me.

Because I didn't want to hate Mitchell. Not again. Not in the way I had at first, when I had learnt of Evie's death, when I had listened to Vi in disbelief; the accident. *She was dead before I got there.*

But it was not just Evie's death that had made me hate him.

It was that, but it was also knowing what had happened between us. Knowing that closeness, that invasion, him right there, in me, only hours earlier. Knowing it and wanting to scratch it out, scrape him out.

And I had told Vi that I hoped he rotted in hell. That I hoped he would die too. Seeing the look in her eyes as I had said those words and knowing there was a part of her that felt that way too, that despite all she preached, she, too, had felt nothing but hate and anger.

And as I said those words, I had seen him, Simon, standing by the door to my room, watching us. Him and Vi looking at each other for just a moment, a moment before Vi opened her arms towards him. Too late. As her arms had opened, he had turned and walked away.

I had hated Mitchell.

And then I had made him fade. Forced him into a series of vague disconnected images, the whole erased.

As I caught Simon's eye, I jerked my head in the direction of the car. I wanted to go now.

211

But Simon did not move. He stood, impassive, silent, staring straight ahead.

I turned, slowly, to look in the direction that he was looking, to follow his gaze across the small group of people, to where Kerry stood, there, on the other side of the grave.

In the quiet that followed the burial, they were all dispersing, walking back towards their cars, muttering low words to each other, some stopping to hug her, some kissing her on the cheek, one or two just standing awkwardly by her side.

I, too, turned to go, to walk away without him, when I saw her separate herself from the group that had gathered around her, when I saw her making her way towards us. In her hand, she still held a flower, a single white lily, pure and creamy, startling against the black of her dress.

Do I know you? She looked uncertain, staring at each of us in turn.

I was about to tell her that she didn't, I was about to make up some story, when Simon began to speak, and as he spoke I found myself staring at him in disbelief.

He told her that she didn't. Know him. Looking down at his feet, scuffing his toes in the dirt, scratching his arm nervously.

But you knew Mitchell?

Clearing his throat, coughing, his voice dry and cracked as he told her that he did. *He came away with us.*

And she continued to look at him, not knowing what he meant. Not knowing what it was that he was trying to say.

On a holiday.

And in the stillness of the morning, I could hear the cars starting, engines turning over, people leaving while we stood there, the three of us, only a few feet separating us from the remaining mourners waiting to say goodbye.

With our family. Years ago.

She did not take her eyes from his. She did not shift her gaze. And the slow crystallisation of awareness, of understanding, hardened.

I think I told Simon to go. I think I tried to pull him away. I do not remember. But I was dragging him, pulling him by the sleeve as she spat at our feet, as she hissed out her words, as she lunged for him, as she told him that he was a *fucking low-down bastard*, as she tried to hit him, restrained by someone, pulled back by another.

All I remember is my brother saying he was sorry. He was sorry. Over and over again.

And as I pulled him towards the car, as I made him get in the passenger seat, as I took the keys from him, I was shouting at him.

And he was crying.

thirty-five

I had no presentiment of disaster. I had no impending sense of trouble.

High in the branches of a peppercorn tree, I did what I had suggested we should do. I waited. With my back against the smooth limbs and my legs stretched out before me, I listened to the rush of the wind off the mountains, now blue in the distance, sighing over the paddocks, the grass gold and rippling in the late afternoon.

I was only fourteen years old.

I looked at my legs. They were thin like a child's. I looked at my fingernails. They were bitten down to the flesh. I looked at the scratches on my arms and the grazes on my knees. I lifted my shorts carefully and looked at the bruise inside my thigh. Deep purple now.

I looked out to where the boulders seemed to roll down towards where I knew the creek bed was, and I continued rewriting the story until it was strong enough to be held up in one piece. I was in love with Mitchell and he was in love with me. And that was the way it was.

When I came back, Vi was sitting on the steps of the verandah, a sherry in one hand, a cigarette in the other.

There was still no sign of the car.

As I sat next to her, she put her glass down by her side.

It's getting dark. She ran her fingers through my hair, picking out leaves, one by one.

In front of us, the shadows were lengthening, the bulk of the house slowly swallowing the lawn, and beyond, the mountains were purple with the last of the light.

I was thinking that maybe I should try and walk into the town, and she stubbed her cigarette out against the cement beneath her feet. *How long do you think it would take?*

I told her I didn't know. *Maybe an hour.*

She tilted her head back and swallowed the remains of her drink. I liked it when it was like this. Just the two of us. Alone. Her not at her typewriter, but here with me. I didn't want her to go.

She squeezed my hand in her own.

They'll be back soon, I told her. And that was what I thought. That they would be back. Soon.

Maybe you're right, and she got up slowly. *Maybe I'll wait a little longer.*

She stood for a moment and looked out across the garden to where the road began. Glowing against the darkening sky, twisting away from us, cutting through the paddocks, until it dipped out of sight into a bend. And as she bent down to pick up her cigarette butt, her glasses slipped, landing on the step next to my foot.

I passed them to her. One lens had fallen out. The other was already taped onto the frame.

I guess I need some new ones now, she said.

And as she turned back towards the house, I heard her repeat my words. *They'll be back soon,* she said, drumming her fingers on the side of her empty sherry glass. *They'll be back soon,* talking more to herself than to me.

But they weren't.

They were not back by the time the sunset had darkened, deep red over the orchard behind us.

They were not back by the time night had slipped in, lavender blackening to ink.

They were not back by the time I gave up on my post and came inside.

And Vi became anxious.

I remember.

I could hear her typing, and then I would hear her stop, listening for the sound of the engine, for the sound of the door slamming, for the sound of footsteps down the hall. Anxious enough to knock the ashtray clattering from her desk to the floor, when we finally did hear it. The sound we had been waiting for: the purr of the motor, the lights through the open door, the footsteps up onto the verandah.

And then we heard the knock.

And as they called out Vi's name, she picked up her papers. She held them in her hands as she walked down that long corridor, while I watched her from the kitchen, the front door propped open with her foot as she talked to them.

The police.

There had been an accident.

Just out of Candelo.

Everything's fine, Vi told me. But I knew she was lying. *I just want you to wait here,* and she had her cardigan, her handbag, and her papers, still there, tight in her hand, as she kissed me goodbye. *I won't be long. I promise.*

And she was gone. The door slamming shut behind her. The sound of the car reversing. The silence.

There was just me. And I was waiting.

Not sure what to do with myself in the enormity of that empty house, wandering from room to room, finally sitting out on the verandah, smoking Vi's cigarettes as I watched the night sky.

While somewhere, out on an empty road, the blue lights of the police car flashed, and Vi watched as they carried Evie's body up from where the car had rolled, tumbling down towards the creek.

And that was all I really knew. Not much, but enough for me to believe the picture that was presented to me. To hold it as truth. Mitchell was drunk. The car rolled. And Evie was dead.

Each stark fact.

Vi holding me tight in her arms and Simon standing at the door to my room.

Me screaming at my brother as he turned and walked away.

Screaming as Vi tried to comfort me, a sour sweet smell, perfume and sweat mingling together as she held my arms close by my side and tried to calm me.

Shhh, she told me, over and over again.

I didn't ask her what had happened to Mitchell.

The flashing lights of the police car, Mitchell bundled into the back.

And as Vi tried to soothe me, I heard the front door slam and Simon walked off into the night.

Sitting by the side of the road with the flowers that he had bought for Mitchell wilting at his feet, Simon buried his head in his hands.

It was some suburban back street, any street in any of these suburbs. The indicator was still clicking, the engine was still on, and the sun was warm through the windscreen.

We were lost.

And as I tried to trace where we were, my finger running aimlessly down the map, Simon spoke.

Can't you see? he said. *It wasn't Mitchell driving. It was me.*

thirty-six

I am not so surprised by the fact that Anton and Louise are moving as I am by the fact that I did not know. That they did not tell me.

Which shouldn't be so unexpected, Lizzie tells me and she is right.

I have avoided Anton, and he has avoided me. He leaves whispered messages on my machine with less and less frequency as he has come to realise that I have no intention of returning his calls. We rarely pass each other on the path, but when we do, we talk politely. Any attempts made by him to vaguely allude to what has happened are so general that it is not difficult to avoid them.

And as for Louise – we do not speak. We have not said a word. Not since the afternoon of the funeral, not since I found her, there on my front step, when I came home. Sitting in the late afternoon sun, watching me as I walked down the path towards her.

When it began with Anton, I never thought about how it

would affect her. I never let myself see her as a person. Not really. She would knock on my door and I would open it to find her standing there, her hair falling into her face, her eyes refusing to meet mine as I would let her in, wanting to hear what she had to say, wanting to know, but not through any genuine concern.

But it was not just her that I failed to see. It was also him. I did not want to know. He would shrug his shoulders and sigh as he told me about each of his impossible love affairs: nights in the Siberian snowfields pining with love for a Russian interpreter, trekking through Sri Lanka with a beautiful married woman, stranded in a castle in Ireland with his best friend's girlfriend. I would hear his tales but I would not hear them. I refused to see myself as the next in line.

And that was not all I refused to see. Because I did not want to see, I did not want to know, that perhaps it was not just boredom that had made me turn towards him. That perhaps I had fallen, tumbled, headlong, into more than I realised.

That perhaps I had fallen in love.

And as I walked towards Louise waiting for me, there, outside my flat, I knew that she knew. Not everything. But enough.

How could you have done it? she asked.

The cool breeze from off the ocean cut through the warmth of the sun.

I looked at my feet, at the cigarette butt Simon had left there that morning, at the weeds growing through the cracks of what was left of the cement, at the dirt and sand that had swallowed most of the path and the garden, at all of this and not at her.

I just don't understand.

As I unlocked the door to my flat, she was there behind me, following me in, wanting me to explain.

I opened the windows wide and let the breeze rush in, lifting my curtains, sending papers scattering across the floor, the leaves of an open book flip-flapping backwards and forwards.

My bed was still unmade, my clothes were thrown across the chair, the sink was piled high with dishes; it was all there, everything that I owned open and on show.

I cleared a space for her to sit, but she did not move. She stayed where she was, leaning against the doorframe, watching me and waiting for an answer.

Did you love him?

No, I told her, still uncertain as to whether I was telling a lie.

Then why did you do it?

I sat down and looked out the window. Out near the horizon, a flock of gulls had circled and alighted, a white flurry on the flat sea. I turned back to face Louise. I could see she had been crying. Her face was white and drawn. Her arms were folded across her chest but despite the defiance in her pose, she was nervous.

I am sorry, I told her. *This is a bad time.*

She was staring at me and I did not go on. She did not want to know. All that had happened, all that I had just learnt from Simon, was no concern of hers. She wanted me to explain, despite knowing that any explanation I gave her would do little to alter what had passed.

I told her I didn't know why I had done it. I hadn't thought. I should have thought. But I hadn't.

I told her there was no excuse.

I told her that he hadn't loved me.

I told her that it had just been one of those things.

And I told her I was sorry.

She stayed where she was, one foot in the door and one foot out, listening to the inanity of my words, trying to dig out some truth, some thread that would make sense to her, or, better still, that would wipe it all away.

What hurts most, she said, and because there was a quaver in her voice, she stopped for a moment. I could hear the intake of her breath, and I waited. *What hurts most is all those times I came to you.*

I remembered. The knock on my door late at night. Telling me she thought he was seeing someone else, but maybe she was just paranoid, maybe she was being ridiculous, maybe she was a little mad; me listening without ever speaking.

Not lying but not telling the truth.

But how could I have told you? I asked her.

She looked at me and she looked away. She was silent.

I could hear Mouse in the bathroom next door. I waited for her to speak.

I guess I knew, she said. *I guess that's why I kept coming to you.*

I didn't understand.

I guess I thought that if I kept coming to you, it would stop you from saying anything. It would stop it from becoming a reality.

And she looked down at her feet.

I got up slowly to close the window and she turned to the door.

Don't, she said, misinterpreting my move, thinking that I was coming to comfort her.

I stopped where I was.

I don't want to make up. I don't want to forgive and forget.

And she did not look back as she stepped out into the last of the day. She did not look back as she turned towards her own flat, and then, changing her mind, headed to the path, leaving me on the doorstep as she made her way past the oleanders and up towards the road.

Standing out there in the cool of the late afternoon, I watched her disappear from sight and I wondered for a moment whether I should go after her.

There was no point.

There was nothing I could say.

From above, I could hear Anton closing the windows. From next door, I could hear Mouse talking to someone.

It was cold but I did not move. I leant against the wall and I closed my eyes. But it was not Louise who occupied my thoughts. Not then. Maybe sometime later. But not then.

It was Simon.

I could not stop thinking about what he had told me. The enormity of it flooding me, overwhelming me.

I needed to speak to my father. I needed him to tell me what he knew.

I heard my phone ring and I heard the click of my answering machine. It was Anton asking me if I was all right.

And I just let him talk.

thirty-seven

It was Bernard who came and picked us up.

Driving to Candelo through the night, keeping himself awake by turning up his stereo another notch and then another, Bach and Dvořák filling the darkness, the palm of his hand beating the steering wheel in time to the ebbs and flows of the music, finally arriving at the house as streaks of dawn threaded through the sky.

I woke early. As I opened the front door, it was his car that I saw first, the new black Porsche sleek and incongruous in the long grass, and I made my way towards it, the freshness of the dew damp through my sandshoes.

He was asleep in the front seat, his mouth open, his face tired and grey.

I tapped on the window, hesitant at first, then loud enough for him to wake.

Honey bunny. It was the name he used to call me when I was little, when he still lived with us, and yet his use of it did not seem out of place, not on that morning.

As he opened the passenger side for me, as I got in next to him, I was crying, and he reached across the seat and pulled me close, soothing me as he stroked my hair off my face. And that was how I wanted to stay but he gently manoeuvred me back into my own seat. *I guess we'd better go in,* he said, and as I nodded my head in agreement, he took my hand, and we walked slowly, in silence, back towards that house.

We were sent to pack. Simon and I, each in our own rooms, the dividing door closed between us.

Most of Evie's clothes were still in her bag.

Most of Mitchell's were spread across the floor.

Our things and theirs.

And we could see each other through the glass doors as we closed zips on bags that neither of us wanted to touch.

In the kitchen, Bernard and Vi sat across from each other, the low hush of their voices occasionally discernible in the quiet that had descended. Bernard wanting to know what had happened, Vi trying to tell him, agitated, tense, irritated with his questions. Was she sure it was Mitchell driving? Was he drunk? Were they both drunk? Where was Mitchell now? Were the police pressing charges? Against whom? Until finally she got up, and, slamming the door behind her, she walked out across the overgrown garden at the back of the house, out towards the orchard, and beyond that towards the paddocks, to where the hills began to roll gently upwards to the windswept mountain country beyond.

My father was only doing what he knew how to do best. Trying to lay out the facts, one by one, trying to assess what practical action, if any, was needed.

And trying to protect your brother. He leant forward and looked at me. There, in his apartment, the day after the funeral, his face almost silhouetted against the flat grey sky.

What you have to understand is that that was my first priority, and he did not take his gaze from mine as he poured himself another wine, before offering the bottle to me.

I shook my head.

Besides, he added, *I really didn't know what to believe. Your brother was distressed. Very distressed.*

And I listened as he tried to explain what had happened and why.

It was Bernard who went to the police, taking Mitchell's bag with him.

We watched him starting the car, Vi and I, and as the engine turned over, we heard the door swing open behind us; we heard Simon's footsteps.

Where's he going? Simon asked.

It was, I think, the first words he had spoken since he had come back with Vi the night before, and I was startled by his voice.

Vi told him he was taking Mitchell's things. To the police.

I watched as the impact of the words hit him, as he leapt down the stairs and ran out across the garden, through the grass, chasing our father's car, his arms waving above his head.

And Bernard stopped, one half of the Porsche still in the grass, the other on the dirt road, as he wound his window down, as Simon leant forward, his head almost completely inside, talking, agitated, anxious, pulling at the doorhandle, the window rapidly wound up, the sound of the engine revving

226

and the cloud of dirt as Bernard disappeared up the road, leaving Simon, standing there. Alone.

He wanted to come with me, and as Bernard continued explaining, I could see he was uncomfortable. He was holding his wine glass between the palms of his hands, rolling the stem backwards, forwards, and backwards again.

We were silent for a moment, neither of us sure what to say, and as I began to ask, I could not bring myself to look at him. *Did he tell you? Did he tell you then?*

I was staring at the table between us, at the mark his glass had left, and I could sense him looking at me, my question there between us.

Yes he did.

And I raised my eyes and met my father's gaze.

So you knew?

He nodded his head. And then, moments later, he shook it. *He was telling me that he did it, that it was his fault, that he wanted to tell the police, and I just didn't know. He was so upset. His sister, your sister, had just died, and of course he felt responsible.*

My father's words trailed off.

Outside, I could see day slowly fading into late afternoon, the shadows of the high-rises lengthening and crossing each other, bringing darkness earlier than it was due.

But you ignored him?

Do you blame me? and he looked at me, directly, challenging me to answer.

I didn't know. It was impossible to know what I would have done in the circumstances. All I knew was that Bernard did what he did.

227

He went to the police station, with Mitchell's one bag on the back seat behind him. He was gone for close to three hours.

It was, he told me on that afternoon in his apartment, *not easy.*

Mitchell had been taken away. He was back in the care of the State. He was awaiting trial. He had, apparently, been protesting his innocence. Over and over again.

Your son told one of the officers that it was 'all his fault'. The sergeant in charge would have looked at my father and my father would not have hesitated in his answer.

Shaking his head sadly, he would have said that Simon was very upset. *He has been blaming himself for having let Evie go with them.*

The policeman would have looked at my father's card. Bernard Rafters, QC. He would have turned it over in his hands. He would have put it back on the desk between them.

It's a terrible business, my father would have said. *You know the boy's,* and he would have hesitated as he searched for Mitchell's name, *Jenkins', history. My wife, my ex-wife, does some foolish things. Taking him away with them was probably the most regrettable of them all.* And Bernard would have shaken his head once more in dismay.

There is no question that my father is a consummate performer. If he had any doubts as to Mitchell's guilt, he would not have let on, not for a moment. The question is whether he did have doubts.

As he talked to me that afternoon, I did not know whether he was, once again, performing. Telling me that he believed

228

Simon was simply distraught and confused, when in fact he knew that Mitchell was innocent.

Bernard asked the police whether they needed to see Simon again. He did not ask directly, of course. He referred to the fact that he wanted to take his family home. That evening, in fact. He assumed there would be no problem.

If the sergeant had hesitated at all, my father would have looked confused. He would have said that they all needed to get back to their lives. They all needed to come to terms with this *terrible tragedy*, and as he spoke he would have begun to make his way towards the door. Surely there could be nothing further?

And the sergeant would also have stood up. *Obviously, if we need your son for questioning?*

Of course, my father would have said, one foot already in the corridor, one hand grasping the sergeant's. *Of course.*

And as Bernard thanked him for his time, he would have told the sergeant to call him. *If you need anything further. You have my card.*

In the intense heat of the afternoon, the main street would have been deserted. The few people who were out would have been down by the river, sitting listless on park benches underneath the shade of the elms. Old people. People passing time.

My father's car was parked outside the police station. A city car. Out of place. Obvious. The fine film of dust coating the black duco doing little to alter the fact that it did not belong on these streets.

And as Bernard unlocked the driver's side, he was aware

that the sergeant was watching him from the window of the station. He turned around and waved, briefly, as he let himself into the car. Just once. Friendly. Casual. And then he drove back along the dirt roads, his windows up, the airconditioning on high, the speedometer just over the speed limit, taking the bends without slowing down, driving back to where we waited for him.

Our bags packed and ready for him to take us home.

As he finished speaking, he put his wine glass down on the table between us. He had drunk two-thirds of the bottle, but it did not appear to have had any effect on him.

And there were no further questions? I asked him.

He shook his head.

I looked down at the fine Persian carpet, crimsons and blues twisting in and out of each other, and I did not know what to say.

We did the wrong thing, I muttered, my words so low that they were barely discernible.

But he heard.

And as he leant forward to speak, there was anger in his voice and impatience. *Tell me,* he asked, *what it is that you would have done in the circumstances. Even if you did have doubts. What would you have done?*

The full resonance of his voice filled the room, silencing me.

No matter what kind of father I may have been, he is my son, and she was my daughter, and there was no pleading in his tone, no asking for understanding, just an angry statement of fact. *What on earth do you expect?*

Outside, a light rain had begun to fall, uncertain, a fine mist balanced on the edge of either abating or building. I could hear the elevator clanking as it slowly made its way up the shaft. People coming home for the evening. I had not brought an umbrella. If I was going to leave, this was the time when I should go.

But my father stretched across the table and held out his hand towards me.

I had, he said, and I could not bring myself to look at him, *no choice,* and he let his hand fall back onto his knee, his eyes still resting on my face.

thirty-eight

Simon and I used to pick flowers for a woman who lived down the road from us.

Coming home from school in the early afternoon, we would stop on our street corner and play handball with the boys who lived next door, hitting the ball back and forth, back and forth, until they were called in for afternoon tea. Bored and restless, knowing that Vi would probably not be home, and if she were, she would be working, we would continue to hit the ball dispiritedly to each other for a little longer.

It would usually be Simon who would first say that he'd had enough. That we should get home.

And do what? I would ask.

Have something to eat, he would answer.

I would look at him.

Stale wholemeal bread, cheese and a few limp radishes in the fridge. Compared to the next-door neighbours' biscuits and cake, it was hardly enticing.

Pulling at a few sweet-smelling twists of jasmine, honey-tipped nasturtiums and daisies, I would start picking flowers for Mrs Hastings.

And Simon would help.

Roses, geraniums, marigolds; we would raid each of the gardens leading down the hill to her front door, until by the time we let ourselves in through her gate, our hands were filled with an extraordinary array of colours.

Mrs Hastings lived on her own. I do not know what happened to her husband. Perhaps he died, perhaps they were divorced. She seemed old to us, terribly old, but now I realise she must have only been in her fifties.

We did like her. And the very first time we took her flowers, our reasons were not self-serving.

We were taking them home to Vi, coming back up the hill with our stolen bouquet, when she stopped us. Leaning over her fence, she told us that daisies were her favourite.

It was Simon who offered them to her.

And she asked us in, filling our now empty hands with the sweets that she kept in her cupboard. Sugared mint leaves, jubes and caramel buttons. Sticky in our fingers.

She had a house full of things. Ships in bottles, wind-up toys, old magazines, different-coloured wool, clutter collecting dust in every corner.

She showed me how to crochet with an old cotton reel.

She gave me bottles of perfume that she no longer used.

And each time we went to leave, she would ask us to stay a little longer, to have some tea, to make sure that we came back soon.

And we did.

Picking the flowers a little more hastily on each occasion, the bunches a little scrappier, a little more wilted, a little less colourful, until one day Simon stopped me.

You can't do that, and he looked at the few leaves and weeds that I was holding in my hand.

I couldn't see what the problem was. *It doesn't matter,* I told him, impatient to get going.

He wouldn't move. He wasn't coming. It was wrong.

I just rolled my eyes and walked off without him, heading down the hill, wanting the sweets she gave us, and any other small treasure that might also fall my way.

But when I got to the gate, I stopped. In my hands, the leaves had begun to wilt, the one dandelion head, white fluff, had blown away leaving only a dry stalk between my fingers.

And as I let them all fall to the ground, I turned around and headed home.

In the weeks that followed the funeral, Simon and I did not talk much.

I don't think either of us knew what to say.

Each time I would find myself about to speak, about to lean forward and say something, the words would dissolve and I would pull back again, open-mouthed and silent.

It was not even possible to ask him the mundane questions I had always asked him. I would try, but in the light of all that was still unsaid, my words would wither in their inanity, leaving me speechless.

Once, closing the front door to my mother's house and stepping out onto the street, I saw Simon walking towards me in the early evening light. I watched him as he slowly made his way up the hill, the afternoon paper tucked under his arm, his too small parka, pale grey and dirty, zipped up to his chin, his eyes fixed on the ground.

He looked up, just as my bus came around the corner, and in the slowness of the moment that followed, I didn't let the bus just go past and stay to talk to him; I turned towards the stop and started walking in that direction, not looking at Simon, but seeing him, his hand frozen in the air, waving at me as I turned my back on him. And as the doors closed with a thud behind me, and the bus pulled out onto the road, I could not bring myself to look back to where he still was, there on the footpath watching me disappear from sight.

I knew then that this was the worst place to which we had descended.

But it was not only him to whom I could not talk. I could not talk to anyone.

I tried with Lizzie, as she drove me home from the clinic. Once again, I found myself without words. Overwhelmed by the enormity of my brother's revelation, I could not bring myself to repeat it out loud. And I changed the topic. Skipping from what I had begun to say to something else, anything, with a speed that made me stumble mid-sentence, and left her looking at me, confused.

What are you talking about? she asked.

Nothing, I said, and she did not question me any further.

I also tried with Marco.

Late one night, after spending the day with Vi, I came home and saw the scrap of paper on which I had written his number on the floor by the side of my bed.

I dialled without thinking.

It rang eight times.

And just as I was about to give up, he picked up the phone.

He was surprised to hear from me.

How are you? We both asked each other the same question at the same time, and we both responded with the same words: *fine, good,* our sentences synchronised in an awkwardness that made me want to hang up without going any further.

He told me he had moved. He told me he had a new job. And he told me he had recently started seeing someone; his words a jumble, a rapid-fire of facts with little behind them other than a desire to let me know that he had been doing well, never better, since we had seen each other last.

And how about you? he asked.

I looked up at the ceiling. *Just the same,* I said. *Just the same.*

And I knew then that I wasn't going to tell him, not even when he asked me if I was calling for any reason, for anything in particular.

No, I said, *I just wanted to see how you were.*

And he told me he was fine, again, and he asked me how I was, again, and I, too, told him I was fine; all our words seeming to have done little more than take us back to where we began.

We hung up, without me having told him a thing.

I sat on the edge of my bed and I looked at the telephone there on the floor.

Apart from Bernard, there was no one with whom I could really speak.

And I needed to talk to someone.

236

I still do.

I just don't know who to go to. I just don't know who I could tell.

Because I am worried about Simon.

And I do not know if Vi should know.

thirty-nine

Mari's picnic is arranged for today.

I offered to make a salad and then wished I hadn't. As usual, there was nothing in the fridge. I am not, as my friends often tell me, very good at taking care of myself.

In the twenty minutes before they are due to arrive, I decide to go up the street and buy something, but just as I am about to close the door behind me, the telephone rings.

It is my friend Lester.

He is calling to let me know that he has finally pulled together the money he needs to make his film.

Where have you been? he asks me. *I keep leaving messages and you never get back to me.*

I tell him I am sorry, I have been busy. *Snowed under.*

He is excited. He wants to give me the lead. *You're perfect for it.*

I am surprised. *Really?* I ask him.

Absolutely, he tells me.

He has talked about his film for so long that I have never

238

really thought it would happen. We arrange to meet tomorrow, and when I finally hang up, I realise I have no time to go to the shops and nothing to take with me.

I am standing by the open fridge door, looking at the few scraps of food and wondering what to do, when I hear him coming down the path.

Simon.

And seeing him walking towards me, the excitement I felt at Lester's news evaporates and the heaviness descends.

Are you ready? he asks, barely looking at me as he stands, awkwardly, on my doorstep.

I tell him I will be a moment. *Come in,* I say, and he does, although it is clear that he would rather stay where he was.

How is she? I ask him, referring to Vi, who has had a bad night, and he shrugs his shoulders as he tells me she is just the same.

When I first learnt that my mother was ill, I found it difficult to believe. I could not remember her ever having been sick.

It was Mari who told me, some months ago.

Vi, she said, *has emphysema.*

It was her hesitancy, rather than the words themselves, that alarmed me.

I'm telling you because your mother is acting like it's nothing. But I thought you should know.

I sat on my bed. I looked out my window. And I asked her how it had happened.

The cigarettes, I guess, and there was a slight break in her voice.

I did not know what to think. I had always equated

239

emphysema with old men, asbestos, mines; an illness closely linked to a cause that Vi would fight, not something that would actually affect her.

I'll come over now. It was all I could think of to say.

Mari told me it was okay. *She just needs to stop smoking, and to rest.*

She spoke calmly, but I could hear the distress in her voice.

I told her I would move home. If she wanted. *Tomorrow,* I offered.

She laughed. *Truly,* she said. *It's all right. But thank you.*

And although the illness has dramatically altered Vi's life, it has not meant the immediate death that I had originally thought. It is a state that we are all learning to live with, a little more each day, sometimes even allowing ourselves to believe what the doctors have assured us is true: that she will be around for a lot longer, that she is not going to die just yet.

Bernard recently asked me if I had discussed all that had happened with Vi, and I shook my head. *How can I?* I asked.

I wanted to know if he thought she knew. If he thought she had always known.

I'm not sure, he said, and when I looked at him, silent, questioning, he became angry. *Honestly,* he said.

He wants me to just let it go. He believes that bringing it up now will not achieve anything.

And in the nights I have sat with my mother, watching bad Hollywood movies, or talking about Evie, I have done as he advises. I have not said a word.

But then Simon comes home.

And when I see him, standing at the door as we talk, or

waiting as he waits now in my flat, I do not know if my silence should continue.

I am trying to find my shoes when I tell him that Mari has been concerned about him, that she has noticed he has been taking time off work. I ask him whether he is all right, but I am not looking at him as I speak.

I'm okay, he tells me.

He is leaning against the doorframe, staring out across the garden. I cannot see his face, but I can see his hand and it is shaking as he brings his cigarette to his mouth, the ash long and slender, trembling on the tip.

Are you sure? I ask as I come towards him, pulling the door closed behind me.

He is wiping at his eyes with the back of his hand, and in the awkwardness of the moment, I do not know what to do. I reach for him and he pulls back, losing his balance, one foot in the garden, as he slides slowly down the wall until he is sitting on my front step, his weight straining against his best jeans, his face red and hot.

Oh, Simon, I say, and it is all I can say, over and over again.

I'm okay, he tells me, trying to pull himself up.

But he can't. He stays where he is, knees to chest, head in his hands.

I am about to speak, I am about to say something, but then I see them all, Evie, Mitchell, Simon, and once again, the words just seem to disappear, and I am taking my hand off his shoulder before I know what it is that I am doing, and I am telling him that I do not know what I am supposed to do, my voice louder than I had intended, sharp and harsh.

I can't deal with this, I say. *I can't.*

And I can see his shoulders shaking, as I keep talking, telling him that I wish he had never told me, telling him that it isn't fair to expect me to carry this too, telling him that it is too much; all the wrong words coming out as he pulls himself up again, and without looking at me, turns, heading away from the path, and through the morning glory, through the lantana, trying to get away, stumbling as I run after him, chasing him.

Wait, I am shouting. *Wait.*

But he doesn't. It is his ankle, caught in the knotted vines, that slows him down, that gives me a chance to catch up.

And we both stand there. At the bottom of the garden, where the stairs lead down the cliff to the sea, smooth and flat under the morning light.

This shouldn't have happened, I think to myself. Not today.

I'm sorry, I say.

He is trying to free his foot, unknotting the twisted leaves and purple flowers that wind their way around his ankle, and I know I have only a few moments to put this right.

Please, I say. *We can't be like this. Not today.*

He does not look up.

I shouldn't have said what I said. And I reach forward, slowly, carefully, to try to help him.

The breeze from off the ocean is cool, and as our fingers brush, I can feel him calm. Just slightly. Together we untwist each of the strands that hold him still, stuck in this spot, piece by piece, until his foot is freed, and we both stand upright and face each other. With his back to the morning light, it is difficult to see his expression, it is difficult to make out the hurt in his eyes, the uncertainty in his mouth, but I know they are there.

I am, however, in full view. My face before him and I want him to see, I want him to know, that the anger has gone, that it is all right. But as I try to keep my eyes on his, I find I can't. I find I am looking at the ground, unable to give the complete reassurance I had wanted to show.

They're waiting for us, I say.

And as he follows me back through the garden and up to the road, I think to myself: I am failing you.

No matter how hard I try, I am failing you.

forty

I do not know what really happened. Not all the details.

Sitting by the side of the road after the funeral, Simon told me he had been driving. That much I do know. That much I can hold to be truth.

The rest I can only guess. Filling in the gaps, imagining how it happened, imagining the chain of events leading up to the car tumbling, turning upside down, toy-like, there at the bottom of the hill, there in the creek, wheels rocking back and forth, back and forth, body crushed like tin, and somewhere inside, Evie, dead on impact.

I was in the bath when Mitchell suggested that they *go for a spin.*

Come on, he urged, *she'll never know.*

Simon, no doubt, would have been hesitant. But wanting to please, wanting it to be just him and Mitchell again, he would have eventually agreed.

He hadn't counted on Evie. Running after them, running across the garden, shouting that she wanted to come too, refusing to take no for an answer, perhaps even saying that she would tell if they left her behind.

And so he let her in. Opening the car door and telling her that she had to be good. She mustn't say a word. Cross your heart. Hope to die.

I guess he thought they'd just go up and down the dirt road a couple of times.

Nothing too risky in that.

Nothing too dangerous.

But that was not how it was.

That was not how it happened.

Mitchell wanted to go further. He wanted to go all the way into town, to buy beer at the pub, to head out along the back roads towards the coast, pulling over to stop and drink; and then he wanted to keep going, to where the surf crashed on the beach, white and salty in the last of the afternoon light.

When Mitchell asked Simon if he wanted to have a go, *to get behind the wheel*, Simon didn't say no. Light-headed and bleary-eyed from the sun and the alcohol, he turned the key in the ignition.

The road was empty. Twisting between the hills, he took each bend slowly at first, but as his confidence built, he began to pick up speed. They had the tape player up loud, the windows open, and the wind was fresh and sweet as they rounded each corner, faster, faster, foot down, screaming with the exhilaration, screaming as they hit each bend, screaming as they neared the next and the next.

And screaming as they tumbled.

As they rolled.

As they hit. The rocks.
There at the bottom.
Wheels still spinning.
And everything silent.

I look at Simon now, sitting next to me in the back seat of Mari's car, and that is what I keep seeing. That afternoon with him as he was then, behind the wheel. All those years ago.

And what is worse is that all I have imagined, the chain of events I have made up for myself, may not even be correct. It may, in fact, have been Simon who suggested they take the car, it may have been Simon who wanted to stop at the pub, it may even have been Simon who insisted that he drive for a while.

I don't know.

And I look away again, staring out the window, trying to stop myself from seeing, eyes fixed on the road, as Mari talks. She knows there is something wrong, and she is angry with us. But she is not going to snap. She is not going to lose her temper. She is not going to let the entire day be ruined. Instead she directs her conversation at Vi, who taps her fingers intermittently on the dashboard, trying to find a use for her right hand now that it can no longer hold a cigarette, her left resting on a pile of clippings, advertisements for houses in the mountains. And as Mari describes each of them, I know the day will be as I had expected it would be. An attempt to make our mother believe that a move would be good for her. Despite the fact that it is clear Vi will not be easy to convince.

For God's sake, she says as Mari asks her to smell the air for the fifth time. *You know how much I hate fresh air,* and she pats Mari's leg to let her know that it is a joke. Just.

Whether you like it or not, it's what you need, and it is evident from the tone in her voice that Mari is offended.

Vi laughs, the throaty laugh she has developed in the last few months, and tells Mari that at sixty-five, she believes she is old enough to now know what she needs and what she doesn't.

Like cigarettes? Mari's mouth closes tight on the word and she glances angrily across at Vi, who refuses to be silenced.

It's certainly what I'd like right now, she says with her usual argumentative defiance.

And as Mari glares at her once more, I find myself looking at Simon, wishing I could roll my eyes in some kind of conspiratorial understanding, but he only looks away.

The first two houses that we stop at are so ugly, Vi refuses to get out of the car.

By the third, Mari has no patience left. *I don't know why,* she says, *I don't know why I bother,* and she pulls over and leans forward, resting her head on the steering wheel.

It is then that Simon decides he has had enough. Opening the door without a word, he gets out, and before any of us really knows what is happening, he starts walking off.

Vi is comforting Mari, telling her to calm down, and as I lean forward to say that Simon has gone, *Hadn't we better go after him?* I realise there is no point.

It's okay, Vi says as Mari cries, heavy tears from months of trying to fight back the fear she feels, the stress and strain of my mother's illness, and I leave them, the pair of them, there in the car by the side of the road.

Simon does not walk fast.

Under the coolness of the autumn sky, he crosses the park slowly, walking without purpose towards the soft blue-grey of the mountains beyond.

I do not call out to him. I do not rush to catch up with him.

In the stillness of the park, I walk just a little faster than him, the bright leaves crisp underfoot, the air fresh and sweet, and I make my way towards him, there, by the war memorial, just ahead of me.

There is a bench underneath an oak tree, half in the sun, half in the shade, and Simon sits, heavy, on one side; I sit on the other.

Are you okay? I ask him.

He looks across at me, and then turns his eyes to the ground.

He does not speak straightaway. Together we listen to the gentle sigh of the wind from the valley below, slowly growing accustomed to the quiet of this place.

I am looking at my feet, scratching a hole in the gravel. *I am sorry,* I tell him, *about this morning,* and as I try to meet his gaze, the sun catches my eye, so that I am forced to squint, and he looks, for just a moment, like the brother I used to know.

I shouldn't have told you. He stares out at the mountains beyond. *I shouldn't have told you.*

We are silent again. I am trying to find the words. I know what they are. But I cannot find them.

Somewhere, in the distance, we hear the slam of a car door. And I know we do not have much time.

Do you think she knows? I ask him, jerking my head back in the direction of the road.

He shakes his head, and then leans forward into his hands. *I tried to tell her,* he says. *I tried,* and as he speaks, I know, now, that Bernard is probably right.

I have to somehow let it go.

Across the park, there is a group of young boys. Sleeves rolled up to their elbows, they try to tackle each other, to throw each other to the ground.

I am watching them. They are so far away, I cannot tell whether it is a game or a fight. One breaks free and I watch as he runs, shouting out to the others, circling them, dodging them as they try to catch him and throw him to the ground.

A glint of blond hair. A checked shirt.

I close my eyes and they are no longer there.

Everything is okay.

And I hear Vi's voice before I see her, making her way towards us, tiny, tottering in her high heels, with Mari right behind her, picnic basket in one hand.

Lunch, she tells us, and as they spread the rug out, right there on the grass, I turn back for one moment, to the other side of the park, to where they were, the boys.

But there is nothing.

Just the trees and the autumn sky.

They have gone.

Time to eat, Mari tells us.

And that is what we do.

CLOSED FOR WINTER

Georgia Blain

Sometimes I wish I could enlarge my photograph so that I could see the details more clearly. I know it is foolish but I think there may be something out there, under the outline of the tin roof, or under those boards, that I have missed . . .

Twenty years have passed since that day on the jetty but it is only now that Elise has found the strength to go back and face the events of her past. And so she begins to unravel all that has been tying her up, picking through that day, piece by piece, from beginning to end. Over and over again.

But sometimes what you uncover is not what you were searching for, and Elise finds herself face to face with a truth she had not expected . . .

Closed for Winter is a gripping novel that will haunt you to the very end, and a powerful, positive story about the pain of letting go.

SING TO ME

Penny Flanagan

When the silence had struck, some five years before, Margaret hadn't cared to dwell on what exactly had caused it. All she had known was that one day she had opened her mouth to sing, and what poured forth was not a pure golden sound that filled empty rooms but the deepest, widest, most aching silence she had ever known in her life.

Once a singer of great promise, Margaret has turned her back on music in an attempt to control a wilful, damaged heart. She exists in a blank cocoon of silence, untouched by passion, until Adrian brings music crashing through the barrier and with it joy and danger . . .

A story about how music makes us fall in love.

THE GOLDEN DRESS

Marion Halligan

There was a picture of her dancing alone, the partner out of shot, her body a slender shapely sheath, her shiny shoes reflecting yellow light, her head thrown back so her hair swirled, her lips smiling. Molly would have known that the smile was furious and heartbroken, but in the photograph it is triumphant.

The image of Molly in her dazzling golden dress haunts three generations. Ivy, who helps Molly sew the dress from a scrap of fabric; Frank, whose love is forbidden; and Ray, who loses himself in the memories of his mother.

When Ray disappears on the streets of Paris, his lover Martine embarks upon a search for him that takes them to unexpected places. Thread by thread, the secrets of his family unravel.

Weaving together the past and present against a backdrop of seascapes, Sydney and Paris, *The Golden Dress* is a rich novel of love and secrets, memories and stories.

'Marion Halligan's magical word pictures have that serene intensity that is now her hallmark.'   ROBERT DESSAIX

TREADING ON DREAMS

Kristin Williamson

In the spring of 1954, in the small seaside town of Skinners Bluff, Anna Danielssen is filled with hope for the future. From the tower of her family's ramshackle house overlooking the sea, she dreams of the world beyond.

Anna's mother, Katharine, is a talented musician, regarded by the locals as eccentric. Her sister Charlotte is beautiful, bored and so desperate to leave home she will marry the first man who asks. The two youngest children retreat to a fantasy world of their own. It's up to Anna to keep the family together – or is it? What of their father, whose name is never mentioned?

With summer approaching, secrets are revealed which will change the family forever. This is the story of a young girl's coming of age, when old dreams are challenged and new dreams discovered.